An Unexpected Doppelgänger

By: Richard Tremblay

To my wife and family, for their love, support and encouragement.

Chapter 1

"Oh my God… Kevin!" The pitch of Anne's voice rose with each syllable as it came through the open sliding doors from the deck. "There's a body down there!"

Kevin joined his wife on the deck, putting on a tee shirt as he approached. "Did you say there's a body?

"Yes… look… by the rocks on the beach," she replied, pointing to a spot fifty feet away.

Kevin immediately took to the stairs, running to the beach, his bare feet leaving footprints on the moist beach sand. Anne cautiously watched from the deck until her husband got closer to the body, then, slowly made her way to his side.

At first look, the body could have been that of an older child or a small man or woman. Lying face down, the person was wearing blue jeans, sneakers and a red hoodie sweatshirt. What appeared to be freshly torn sections of the person's clothes were tinged with blood.

Anne arrived just as Kevin moved the body attempting to distinguish if it was male or female. When Kevin turned the body over, his eyes opened wide, and he stumbled backward, falling into a seated position on the sand. Even with severe bruises covering her face, there was no doubt this young woman looked a lot like Anne.

Training and instinct quickly replaced Anne's initial shock and the registered nurse inside her began checking for signs of life.

"Kevin! Call 9-1-1!" Anne yelled, tossing her cell phone in his direction. "I feel a pulse. It's weak, but it's there!"

Minutes later, the sounds of sirens approaching 24 Ocean Edge Drive drowned out the seaside sounds of screeching seagulls and breaking waves. When the sirens stopped, Kevin and Anne looked toward the cottage to see two paramedics with a stretcher, and a young police officer running toward the rocky breakwater where they waited near the young woman. The sights and sounds of emergency vehicles on this quiet dead end street caused several curious neighbors to come out onto their decks, hoping to learn the cause of the commotion.

"She has a slight pulse, and her breathing is very shallow," Anne informed the lead paramedic.

"Thanks… Officer Rousseau will want to speak with you," he replied, as he gestured towards the cottage with a nod of his head.

Kevin and Anne looked back in that direction, and saw Harbor Point police officer, Marc Rousseau approaching.

"Hello… I'm Officer Rousseau. I understand you found the body," he said. Rousseau, a five-year veteran of the force still had a hint of a French-Canadian accent, even though his family had moved to Maine from Quebec when he was in middle school.

"Yes," Anne replied, "when I looked at the beach from our deck this morning, she was lying right where she is now. My husband and I ran here to check it out."

"You live over there, Mrs…?" The officer asked pointing towards the house with his pen.

"Burke. We're Kevin and Anne Burke," Kevin answered.

Continuing his questioning, the officer asked, "When you arrived at the scene, Mr. Burke, what did you see?"

Kevin described how he came down to the beach after Anne had noticed the body, and how he had turned the body over to see the face. He hesitated for a moment, and then added that Anne had then begun to check the body for vital signs.

Kevin's pause caused the young officer to look up from his note pad.

"You hesitated for a moment, Mr. Burke, is there anything else you want add? Did you notice anything unusual?"

"Well, it's just that… it's just that, when I looked at her face, I thought she looked like my wife."

By now, other officers of the Harbor Point, Maine, Police Department had arrived on the scene to investigate, including Detective Sergeant Warren Wilson, Harbor Point's only plainclothes detective. Tall, physically fit, and handsome, only the slight graying of his hair gave a hint of his age. In most police departments, Wilson would have "made captain" by now, but in a small town like Harbor Point, promotions happened infrequently. His last opportunity for promotion before retirement would be at the end of the year, when the Captain Peter Rudman retired from the department. Everyone at the station knew Wilson was the right man to succeed Rudman.

"What do we have, Marc?" Wilson asked as he joined the officer and the Burkes on the beach.

Turning his attention to the seasoned detective, Rousseau rattled off the facts, reading from his notebook.

"We have an unidentified white female, 18 – 25 years of age, auburn hair, blue eyes, approximately five feet, five inches tall. She is wearing blue jeans, sneakers and a red hoodie sweatshirt." Pointing to Kevin and Anne with his pen, he said, "The Burke's noticed her lying on the rocks at approximately 0840 Hours. They called 9-1-1 at 0845."

The senior paramedic interrupted Rousseau's report, "She's alive, Sergeant. She's not responsive, but she is alive. We've stabilized her, and we're going to take her to County Hospital now."

Walking toward the other paramedic and the woman, now on a stretcher, Sergeant Wilson asked, "You didn't find any identification?"

"Nothing definitive," replied the senior paramedic. "She didn't have a wallet or any ID on her. Only this piece of jewelry we removed from around her neck," he said, displaying a locket on a gold necklace chain in his latex gloved hands.

"Give it to me" Wilson replied, "I'll make sure it is kept as evidence, it may help us identify her if no one steps forward. For now, she's a Jane Doe."

Wilson turned looking down at the badly bruised face of the victim, and then back at Anne. Despite the black and blue marks on her face, he noticed it too. Her auburn hair and smooth complexion with a slight freckling about her small, straight nose, gave her a remarkable resemblance to Anne Burke.

"Do either of you recognize her?" he asked, turning back to the Burkes.

"No. We've never seen her before," Anne answered, "and we've been staying at the cottage for the past week. We're on our honeymoon."

"When are you planning to leave Harbor Point?" asked Sergeant Wilson pointedly.

"We have another week, but this beach house belongs to my family. We come here often, especially when my father, Dick McDonald is up here," answered Anne.

"Oh, so your Mac's daughter?"

"Yes… how do you know my father?"

"Mac and I were in the Air Guard together. I remember meeting you and your sister at the base air shows. You were about three, and I think your sister had just finished middle school. I didn't realize Mac kept this place after your mother…"

"Left us?" Anne said with a touch of sadness, finishing Sergeant Wilson's sentence.

"I was so sorry. Your father took it very hard."

Anne sighed, "It took years for Dad to get over it. Luckily, my sister was old enough to help around the house. Without her, I don't think Dad could have survived."

"Did anyone in the family ever hear from your mother?" Wilson asked.

"No," replied Anne, looking down. "Never. Not even at Christmas, or on our birthdays. Apparently she wanted nothing to do with us."

Reaching into his left shirt pocket, Sergeant Wilson said, "Here is my card. If you think of anything, give me a call. Be sure to give your contact information to Officer Rousseau. I'll be in touch."

Wilson nodded good-bye, and headed back toward his cruiser, leaving Kevin and Anne with Officer Rousseau.

After giving the officer their contact information, Kevin and Anne returned to the cottage in silence. When they reached the house, Anne remained on the deck, while Kevin showered and dressed. He joined her a half hour later, offering Anne a cup of hot coffee. She took the cup, simply saying "thanks," not looking up. Instead she kept her eyes on the spot on the beach where they had found the unidentified body.

They sat together in silence for what seemed like an eternity. Finally, Anne broke the silence, asking questions, but not waiting for answers. "I wonder how she got there? I wonder who she is? The fact that she looks so much like me is strange, isn't it? I wonder how she's doing?"

Kevin looked over at her, taking the final swallow of coffee from his mug. "I don't know Annie," he said, using his pet name for her. "Her clothes were wet, so she was in the water at some point. I checked the tide chart before I came out here. High tide was at 7:45 this morning, so if she washed ashore, it must've been after that. She hadn't been there that long when you noticed her. The police in this town are good. I'm sure they'll put every effort into finding out who she is."

"I sure hope so. I keep thinking about her. Maybe we can check with Sergeant Wilson later."

"Sure. Let's take a walk to The Point; do some shopping and grab a bite to eat. When we come home, we can give the sergeant a call."

"Sounds like a plan, honey. It'll help get my mind off her for a bit."

Chapter 2

Joan was extremely proud of her daughter. Sitting in the university's Canfield Courtyard with fifteen hundred friends and family members, she anxiously awaited her daughter's name to be announced. Smart, beautiful, and curious, Emily Elizabeth Fitzgerald was graduating summa cum laude from Stanford Law.

Three years ago, when Emily received her undergraduate degree, the commencement speaker was Tom Brokaw, the former NBC Nightly News anchor and author of *The Greatest Generation*. Joan remembered how inspiring his speech was, and how he challenged the graduates that day, to be the next, great generation.

Today's speaker, however, was a different story. Professor Etienne Pilotte, was a self-centered law professor so arrogant, students often referred to him as "Pompous Pilotte." The professor droned on and on about how "if he were" in these graduates shoes, "he would" use "his" newly minted JD to improve the lives of "the ninety-nine percent."

Joan thought otherwise. After seven years of ridiculously expensive tuition and eating Ramen Noodles twice a day, she figured most of these graduates were more interested in focusing on improving their own lives at this point. Emily was already on her way, having landed a coveted position at Greene & Greene, one of the top law firms in Eagle. Once she passed the bar exam, she would officially be an associate in its family practice division.

As "Pompous Pilotte" continued, Joan reminisced about her own life. The first thirty years sucked. There was no other way to describe it. Her life began badly and went downhill from there. Joan's mother died in the delivery room from complications during childbirth. Her father, having no interest in raising two children alone, left Joan and her older brother with his elderly mother and was never heard from again. When Grandma Alice died six years later, Joan and her brother became wards of the state. They were separated, with Joan living in a string of eight different foster homes. By the time she turned eighteen, Joan had been sexually abused by several of her "fellow fosters," and had spent time in Juvenile Detention for selling drugs. She earned a GED while in "Juvy," and studied nursing at the local community college after being released.

Joan thought she had finally turned her life around when she married Ron Fitzgerald, the assistant manager at the local grocery store. Their first year of marriage was wonderful. Unfortunately, the only luck Joan had was bad luck, and eventually that happiness evaporated. After three failed pregnancies, Joan no longer had any interest in intimacy, causing her marriage to crash and burn. Frustrated, Ron had an affair with one of his cashiers, who quickly got pregnant. Joan remembered signing the divorce papers on her thirtieth birthday.

The sound of applause as "Professor Pompous" concluded his speech brought Joan back to the present. As they began to confer the degrees, Joan joined the other parents trying to get the best vantage point to take a picture with her camera.

Emily's row stood and began walking toward the stage.

"Daniel Marshall Field… Katelynn Jessica Fischer… Samuel Leonard Fishman…"

She's next, Joan thought, stepping forward with her camera poised to record this important moment in both of their lives.

"Emily Elizabeth Fitzgerald…"

While the many other graduates received extra applause generated by extended families in attendance, the announcement of Emily's name was followed only with a polite smattering of congratulatory applause from the audience, and the sound of her mother's voice yelling, "Congratulations Emily!"

Emily was accustomed to this, of course. With Joan her only living relative, celebrating the milestones in her life had been rather small affairs. Typically, her mother would take her out to dinner at a chain restaurant like Olive Garden, and then give her a greeting card with a personal check enclosed.

She had friends, of course, and even an occasional boyfriend, but for some reason these relationships never lasted more than a year. Joan always kept her close. When Emily was young, she thought it was because her mother was being overprotective, wary of losing the only person in her life. As she got older, however, Emily suspected that somehow, her mother was the reason she never had any close relationships growing up. Things got really ugly when it came time to select a college. Joan had been so angry and disappointed when Emily did not accept the invitation to attend Boise State. For Emily, it was an easy decision. A full-ride scholarship at a prestigious university often referred to as "the Harvard of the West," or paying in-state tuition to a university known more for its football team, and its blue stadium turf.

Walking back to her seat, Emily told herself, "*Your* life begins now. Make it your own!" Her mother did not know it yet, but Emily had already rented an apartment in Eagle, about twenty miles from the condo her mother thought she would once again share with her daughter after seven years of college in California.

Following the ceremony, Joan found Emily sharing congratulatory hugs with several of her fellow graduates.

"Congratulations, Sweetheart! I'm so proud of you," Joan said as she hugged her daughter. "I found an Olive Garden in town. Let's go celebrate your graduation in-style!"

Really? In-style? Emily thought. Over the past seven years, she had experienced many 5-star Italian restaurants in Silicon Valley, which made Olive Garden look like a fast food restaurant in comparison. But, Emily knew it was her mother's favorite, so she acquiesced, especially since she needed to break the news to her mother about the one-bedroom apartment she had rented near her new place of employment.

An hour later, they were eating salad and breadsticks while waiting for their entrees.

"So, are you packed and ready to move back home to Caldwell?" Joan asked, excitedly.

"Yeah. I'm renting a small U-Haul trailer tomorrow. I should be able to fit seven years' worth of stuff in the trailer and my Jeep."

Leaning in closer, as if revealing a secret, Joan said, "Before I left, I redecorated your room, and cleared a corner of the basement to make room for all of your college stuff. Everything is ready for you to move back in!"

Emily waited for the server to finish placing their entrees on the table, before telling her mother about her new apartment.

"Mom, I won't be moving back to Caldwell with you."

"But, I repainted the walls, hung new curtains, and bought a new bedspread," Joan replied, adding, "It looks very nice! I even bought a nice bookcase from IKEA for all of your law books!"

"It sounds wonderful Mom, but I've rented a one bedroom apartment in Eagle, not far from G Squared."

"G Squared? What's that? Some dance club?" sputtered Joan.

"No Mom. It's how people at the firm refer to Greene & Greene."

"That's silly. Just like the idea of you moving out on your own."

"Mom, I've been on my own for the past seven years. What's the difference?

"You were just away at college… living in college housing."

"Mom… I'm a twenty-five year old college graduate, who also happens to be a lawyer now. It's time for me to get my own place."

"Well, it's not happening Emily. And that's final!"

"I've already signed a lease agreement. IT IS HAPPENING, MOTHER," Emily said, accentuating each word.

"I suppose you want your own place just so you can have _sex_, any time you want," Joan said in a slightly raised voice.

People eating at nearby tables glanced in Joan's direction, with one woman nearly choking on her spaghetti upon hearing the comment.

"Mother!" Emily exclaimed.

Following that exchange, the two women finished their entrees in an awkward silence that continued until Joan parked her rental car on the street in front of Emily's student apartment.

"Well, I imagine you still have some packing to do Emily. I have a plane to catch. Will I get to see you when you get back to Idaho?"

"I thought you were flying home tomorrow afternoon, Mom?"

"I've decided to take an earlier flight. It sounds to me like you big shot lawyers at "G Whatever-you-call-it," need your privacy."

"Mom. That's not what I meant, and you know it. I didn't mean to hurt your feelings."

"I'm sorry Emily, but you managed to completely ruin what started out as an excellent day."

"Don't you think you're being a little dramatic, Mother?"

Ignoring the comment, Joan said, "I've got to go." Reaching into her purse, she took out a greeting card-sized envelope. "Here's your present. Congratulations."

"Thank you, Mom. You didn't have to do this," Emily said opening the envelope.

"I didn't have to do a lot of things, young lady, but I did them for you. It was always *for you.*"

"Then you understand why I'm doing this Mom. I'm doing this for you. Now you can move on with *your life.*"

"That's the biggest load of bullshit, I've ever heard, young lady. You'll make a fine lawyer."

Emily sat there in shock. She'd never heard her mother talk like that before. After a few more seconds of awkward silence, Joan said. "I've got to get to the airport. I'll see you, whenever. Please call before you come over. I don't want you simply dropping by whenever you feel like it."

Seconds later, Emily stood alone on the sidewalk with her diploma and a large tote bag in hand. *All righty then…That went well*, she thought sarcastically, watching her mother speed away, running a red light in the process.

* * * * *

"I can't believe she's not moving back in with me," Joan kept muttering to herself, as she made her way through airport security. One TSA agent, noticing she was talking to herself, stopped her to ask if she was okay.

"Of course, I'm okay," barked Joan. "Just because my daughter no longer wants to live with me doesn't mean *I'm* the crazy one!"

Watching Joan trundle down the concourse toward her flight's assigned departure gate, the TSA agent rolled her eyes at her partner, as if saying, "Yeah lady. You're not crazy."

"I'll call the United gate agent and give her a heads-up on that one," her partner volunteered in agreement.

Joan arrived at the departure gate with plenty of time to spare. Her flight was not scheduled to leave for another ninety minutes. Sitting in the gate waiting area, she reached for the Danielle Steele novel she had started on the flight to San Francisco. Although she tried to read, Joan found it difficult to concentrate on the story. Her conscience kept returning her to an incident when her life changed forever.

After receiving her nursing degree, Joan had a difficult time finding a full-time job in a hospital because of her criminal record for selling drugs. To make ends meet, so took a few additional courses and became an Emergency Medical Technician, working for the local ambulance company.

That morning, Joan and her partner, Michael Young responded to a two-vehicle accident near downtown. Arriving at the scene, they learned the woman had been driving through the intersection when a teenaged driver ran a red light, squarely hitting the driver's side of her car. The impact sent the woman's car careening across the intersection, and sent the unrestrained teenager through his windshield. First responders found the young man's body atop the roof of the woman's car. Luckily, the car's frame absorbed most of the impact, saving the life of the woman and her unborn baby.

Joan contacted the emergency department of St. Luke's Regional Medical Center, advising they were preparing to transport a pregnant Caucasian female, 35 to 40 years old, suffering from severe head trauma as well as multiple cuts and bruises.

"Please save my baby! Do whatever it takes to save my baby," the woman said to Joan, before blacking out.

Joan examined the mother and noticed the accident had induced labor. She could see the baby's head crowning. This was not the first baby Joan had delivered. In fact, she had delivered more babies than any other of her fellow paramedics, earning her the nickname "The Stork."

With lights flashing and sirens wailing, Michael adeptly guided the ambulance through traffic toward the hospital while Joan worked on their passenger.

After delivering the healthy baby girl, Joan noticed a second, smaller baby was hiding behind its slightly larger sibling. Working quickly, she delivered the second child, another girl.

Joan remembered what the woman kept saying, "Save my baby… save my baby."

Is it possible she didn't know she was having twins? Joan thought. It's possible given how they were positioned.

Then something clicked in Joan's head. Her dark side was now in control. Looking to see if Michael noticed the birth of the second baby, she hid the tiny newborn in her now empty lunch cooler. When they arrived at the hospital, Joan had Michael deliver the young mother and her newborn to the trauma team waiting inside.

"Can you take them inside, Michael? I'll stay here and clean up this mess and complete the paperwork before Stacey relieves me. She should be here soon."

Working quickly, Joan cleaned the ambulance's interior, bagging all of the biohazard material into the appropriate red bags. She checked on hidden Baby Number Two and completed the paperwork just as Michael returned with the gurney.

"They stabilized the mother, and the doctor said her baby girl will be okay too. Nice work Joan!"

"Shit, I forgot to give you her purse when you brought her in, Michael. I'm sure they'll want her information. I'll go give it to them. What exam room is she in?"

"She's in four," Michael replied, as he watched the very attractive Stacey Leonard approach.

"Hey guys! Looks like you've had a busy day," Stacey said.

"Hi Stace," Joan said. "You ready to relieve me?

"I suppose so," she replied, looking up at the cloudless, cobalt blue sky. It's such a nice day; I'd rather be jogging along the Greenbelt."

As Joan and Michael nodded in agreement, dispatch was calling on their radios.

"Sounds like you've got places to go guys," Joan said. "I'm off tomorrow. See you Wednesday."

With that, Michael and Stacey were off on their next call.

Joan looked in on the tiny baby inside her cooler before entering the hospital to drop off the woman's purse. The little one was sleeping. She'd need some attention soon. Luckily Joan had the rest of the afternoon, and the rest of her life to take care of her new daughter.

Chapter 3

"The Point" was the town's tourist commercial center, catering to the thousands of summertime visitors who came to Harbor Point Beach for the day, the week, or the season. Ocean Drive and Atlantic Avenue had everything people on vacation wanted - gift shops, tee shirt shacks, and small nooks to buy fudge, fried dough, and salt water taffy. Once the sun went down, crowds were drawn to "The Point" by the aroma, sights, and sounds coming from small bistros, nightclubs, and the arcade.

The Ocean House, a Victorian-era grand hotel, sat on the bluff overlooking "The Point." Considered the "grand-dame" of hotels in that part of Maine, it shared the scenic coastline with several B & B's that opened from May to October. Guests of the Ocean House enjoyed the panoramic ocean views from the wrap-around veranda. Luckily, the hotel's restaurant, Victoria's, was open to everyone. Tables on the veranda made it the perfect place for a light lunch or an elegant dinner when the weather cooperated.

Today was a beautiful day. The morning's fog had burned off leaving the cobalt blue sky unblemished by clouds. A light sea breeze tempered the hot August sun as Anne and Kevin walked hand in hand along Shore Drive on their way to The Point. Stopping occasionally to look out at the Atlantic Ocean, they watched families build castles in the sand and teenagers playing volleyball on the strip of sandy beach.

Taking a left onto Atlantic Avenue at the Community Church, Kevin commented on the message sign announcing the title of that weekend's sermon. "'Exposure to the SON, Can Keep You from Burning.' That's a clever sermon title for a church at the beach," he said with a chuckle.

Anne replied, "The Reverend has been using that line every summer for the last ten years."

"I'm getting hungry," Kevin said. "How 'bout Victoria's… my treat?"

"Sounds good to me," Anne said. "I'm in the mood for their grilled chicken garden salad."

Fifteen minutes later, they were sitting at their veranda table, sipping iced tea while waiting for their food.

"Have I ever taken you to visit Harbor Point Light?" Anne asked, as she gazed out toward the lighthouse in the distance.

"You were going to take me there the first time you brought me to Harbor Point Beach," Kevin said, "but something else came up, and we never made it."

"Something else came up?" she asked, tilting her head quizzically.

"Ooooh yeah…" Kevin replied mischievously.

Anne responded with a swipe at Kevin's shoulder, adding, "Well, we'll just have to go some day this week."

Kevin pointed out the three tour boats cruising around the light. "It's quite a draw isn't it?"

"It's one of the most photographed lighthouses in the country," Anne said as their plates arrived.

A low flying helicopter appearing from the north captured everyone's attention as it followed the coastline southward. The local TV station's news chopper was definitely going somewhere in a hurry, no doubt to cover some breaking story.

Anne's cell phone began to ring, causing some of the other patrons to gaze in her direction with annoyed looks. Taking the hint, Anne excused herself and walked away from the dining area as Kevin kept a watchful eye on her.

"Hello?" she asked with a question in her voice, as she did not recognize the number flashing on the screen.

"Mrs. Burke? This is Sergeant Wilson of the Harbor Point Police Department."

"Hello Sergeant." she answered.

"Are you at your cottage?" he asked.

"No, we're at The Point having lunch. We were planning to call you later this afternoon. Do you have any news?"

"Well, sort of… I just wanted to let you know that word of your finding a Jane Doe on the rocks this morning has already reached the media. The Portland TV stations are calling this a 'breaking story.' A number of stations have already asked me to do on-air interviews. I've sent two additional officers to your place to assist Officer Rousseau in maintaining order."

"That explains why we just saw News Chopper 7 fly by."

"Needless to say," Sergeant Wilson warned, "The reporters will be staking out your place wanting to get comments from you and your husband."

"What should we do?"

"Continue enjoying your day. I have to give them the standard, *'We're still investigating the matter, so there is not much we can comment about the case at this time'* line. That will leave them wanting more, however, so they may try to find you. My advice is to simply tell them you found the body of a young woman, you called the police, and they are investigating."

"I understand. Any word on the girl, yet Sergeant?"

"Last report has her as stable, but she is still unconscious. She must have hit the rocks pretty hard. If you have any problems with the media, let us know. As I said, we have a car at your place to keep an eye on things."

"Thank you, Sergeant. Good-bye."

"You're welcome, Mrs. Burke. Talk to you soon. Good-bye."

Anne closed her phone, and returned to the table.

"Who was that?" asked Kevin.

"That was Sergeant Wilson. He wanted us to know that the media has learned about the Jane Doe, and are reporting the story from our beach. The news helicopter must have been heading there. He told me they sent a police car to keep an eye on things," she explained, recounting her conversation with the sergeant.

Within seconds of each other, both of their cell phones rang. Again, customers on the veranda looked their way, some shaking their heads in disgust.

Anne and Kevin both checked the caller IDs.

"Your father," announced Kevin, looking at Anne.

"Mary Beth," Anne said, holding up her phone. "They must have heard the news too."

"Hi Mac," Kevin said, answering his phone as he left money on the table to cover the meal and tip. *So much for a quiet lunch*, he thought to himself.

"Everything is alright," Kevin said in reply to his new father-in-law's question. "Annie's fine. When we woke up this morning, she walked out onto the deck to see the beach, and that's when she saw the body over by the rocks. We called the police. An old friend of yours from the Guard responded, a Sergeant Wilson."

Anne's father, Dick "Mac" McDonald, had been a pilot in the New Hampshire Air National Guard for most of Anne's life, retiring as a lieutenant colonel the same year she graduated from nursing school. While flying air-refueling missions for the Guard on weekends, Mac flew "puddle jumpers" for a local commuter airline, also based at the Pease International Trade Port in nearby Portsmouth, New Hampshire. Mac had met Staff Sergeant Warren Wilson when Wilson was a member of the Guard's Air Police Squadron.

Meanwhile, Anne had returned to her previous spot on the veranda to speak with her older sister Mary Beth, who had heard about the finding of a "Jane Doe" at their beach on the local news.

"Hi, Mary Beth... Yeah, we're okay. When we woke up this morning, we noticed a body lying in the rocks by the breakwater. She was barely alive. Kevin called 9-1-1. The paramedics came and took her to County Hospital. That's all we really know, Mary Beth. She didn't have any identification with her. The strange thing though, is that she looks like me!"

"Are you sure you're okay?" Mary Beth asked. "It must've freaked you out to find someone on the beach like that?"

"Not really. I see injured people in the hospital all the time. I keep thinking about her though, especially since we don't know who she is, or where she came from. It made me think of Mom. Perhaps something like that happened to Mom, and she lost her memory, and..."

"Anne," Mary Beth interrupted, "Get real. You're a registered nurse. You know those types of things only happen in Lifetime Channel movies!"

Mary Beth Mason was Anne's only sibling. Twelve years her senior, Mary Beth had no choice but to become a surrogate mother for three-year old Anne when their mother Betsy, abandoned the family twenty-five years ago.

Betsy had left young Anne with a next-door neighbor that May afternoon, saying she had to run a quick errand. When Mary Beth arrived home from school, she saw the note her mother left telling her to pick up Anne from Mrs. Gorman, which she did. Mary Beth got concerned, though when several hours had passed and their mother had not returned.

When the girls' father came home that evening he had expected supper on the table - not a note on his dresser. The note stated only that she was leaving - no explanations - no reasons - no forwarding address. The Exeter, New Hampshire, Police found Betsy's 1980 Chevy Citation in the parking lot of the local IGA grocery store later that evening. A thorough investigation followed, including a polygraph test taken by Mac. Nothing they found led them to believe that any foul play was involved. Authorities officially listed Betsy McDonald as a missing person. At that point, Mac hired a private investigator, a former policeman he knew. The ex-cop worked the case for about a year, tracking down every possible lead, but he too came up empty. Someone in town had even started a rumor that aliens had abducted Betsy. Exeter had a history with UFOs, including an incident in the mid-sixties, when several people claimed to have seen a UFO. That spawned a two-part story in *Look* Magazine at the time. Another local couple, Betty and Barney Hill, made news back then too, claiming creatures from a UFO abducted them. These incidents only added to the "water-cooler" speculation by local residents.

Memories, rumors around town and nasty comments by kids in Mary Beth's school made life in Exeter uncomfortable for the McDonald Family. By the time Anne was ready to enter elementary school, Mac had moved the family to nearby Portsmouth.

Twenty-five years had passed, and while the McDonald family had moved on for the most part, Mac, never remarried. He had a few short-term relationships, but nothing ever reached the serious stage. His life was his work and his two daughters.

Mary Beth was only fifteen when Betsy left. She transferred to Portsmouth High School when they moved, and sacrificed participating in many extra-curricular activities in order to help her dad take care of Anne and the house. At first, Mary Beth didn't mind, but after a while, she felt Mac took her for granted, and she began to resent it, especially when she couldn't get into the college of her choice due to mediocre grades; grades she blamed on having to take care of Anne.

Mac, on the other hand, treated Anne like a princess. He did everything he could to make up for the fact that her mother had abandoned the family. Anne excelled in high school, and attended Northeastern University in Boston to study nursing. In her sophomore year, she met Kevin Burke, a Northeastern pharmacy student from Chicago. They quickly became best friends, but it was not until Kevin's then girlfriend gave him the "it's me or her" ultimatum, that Kevin and Anne became a couple.

Kevin and Anne established each of their careers before getting married. His uncle owned an independent drug store in Kittery, Maine, and in anticipation of his retirement, Uncle Liam brought Kevin into the business, with the promise of giving Kevin the first right of refusal to buy the pharmacy in five years.

Anne went to work at the Barbara Bush Children's Hospital at the Maine Medical Center in Portland. She loved taking care of young children and found her job very fulfilling.

Mary Beth's life was not so rosy. She married Dan Mason, her high school sweetheart shortly after graduation, and she waited tables at Yoken's, a well-known Portsmouth landmark. Her husband followed in his father's footsteps working as a lobsterman. Unfortunately, Dan began drinking, which made keeping a job increasingly difficult, and life at home anything but pleasant. Several separations eventually ended in divorce after a twenty-year marriage. They had a daughter, named Sally, and a son named Drew, after New England Patriots quarterback, Drew Bledsoe.

Things only got worse for Dan after the divorce. Following a series of low paying, part-time jobs, he finally found steady work. It wasn't exactly the greatest place to work, but the tips were okay and they paid every week. When things were going well, Dan picked up the kids on Sundays, and kept them until Wednesday. When things weren't going well, they were lucky to see him at all.

Mary Beth eventually accepted her place in life, no longer resenting her father and baby sister, although the little green monster of envy occasionally made an appearance when she compared her life to that of her sister's. Dan, however, never forgave his former father-in-law for showering Anne with attention and money.

Chapter 4

Shoes. Disinfecting shoes. This is what had become of his life. Working in an old bowling alley, handing out "size eights" and "size nines." Even with "pulling doubles," by tending bar at night in the alley's Ten Pin Pub, he was barely making ends meet. He chuckled to himself at the thought though. A recovering alcoholic serving drinks to people, many who were now his friends. *Hey, why not? Sam "Mayday" Malone did it on Cheers, right?* His friends even called him "Sam," even though that was not his real name.

Like Sam Malone, he used to be "a somebody." Then he met "Jim Daniels," and the downward spiral began. Now sober for the past six months, he realized it had been hard on his family, but they had turned their backs on him. He rarely saw his kids, only occasionally exchanging emails or comments on Facebook with them. *At least they hadn't "un-friended" him yet.* His "ex" used to call him when the child support checks bounced, but since the state began garnishing most of his wages for support a year ago, they never spoke. Was he bitter? Yeah, you bet he was. No matter what he did for her, it was never good enough. *It's hard to "keep up with the Joneses," when the Joneses are "perfect."* But they weren't perfect. He knew that then and even more so now, especially with the little secret he recently learned from one of his attractive, young female bar patrons.

Jenny Sullivan was a regular at the Ten Pin Pub. She started coming in every Wednesday night after she and her friends from work bowled in the Office League. Her all-girl team of young accountants called, "The Figures" did very well in the standings, but not because of their ability to knock down more pins than other teams. They typically won, because they knew how to use their "advantage" in the mostly male co-ed league. "The Figures" wore black spandex leggings, and colorful bowling shirts that accentuated their assets. Rather than concentrate on their own lanes, the other bowlers would more often than not, study "The Figures."

While the attention "The Figures" received was nice at first, Jenny eventually tired of being hit-on several times each week, so she began to sit at the bar and chat with the handsome bartender everyone called "Sam." He knew why she sat on the corner stool, and would often run interference when he could tell she was really bothered by the male customers. Jenny and "Sam" quickly became friends, and soon she began coming in after work on non-league nights just to talk and enjoy a glass of Barefoot Moscato wine. "Sam" thought she looked just as good in her business suit, and he loved receiving attention from such an attractive young woman.

One evening, Jenny stopped by the bowling alley after attending an all-day seminar on the campus of the University of New Hampshire in nearby Durham.

"Hey Sam. Didn't you mention once that your ex-wife was a bookkeeper?"

"Yeah, I may have mentioned her to you once or twice. Last I knew she was doing the books for the Ace Hardware in Dover. Why?"

"I think I met her at an accounting conference today. Is her name Mary Beth?"

"Yeah. How'd you meet her?"

"We were seated at the same table, and we started talking. You know… girl talk."

"Did she mention me?"

"Not really, but once I thought I knew who she was, I didn't mention you either. By the way, is her mother a bookkeeper, too?"

"Her mother?" snorted Sam. "Her mother left the family twenty-five years ago. Just disappeared. They found her car in the IGA parking lot but never found her. Mary Beth's father eventually petitioned to have her declared dead. The bastard used the insurance money to send his precious "Princess" Anne to Northeastern. And get this. The sonofabitch never even offered Mary Beth a dime! Can you believe that shit?"

"No, I can't," replied Jenny, sadly shaking her head.

"I'm sorry Jenny. It just pisses me off when I think about how he did everything to please Anne, but always took my ex for granted. She pretty much gave up everything to help raise her little sister after her mom disappeared."

After a few minutes of silence, "Sam" asked, "So what's this about Mary Beth's mom? Did you meet a ghost too?"

"No," Jenny replied. "But during one of the morning breaks, your ex suddenly acted as though she saw one. We were talking when Mary Beth apparently spotted this older woman over my shoulder heading toward the rest rooms. She suddenly jumped from her seat, and started walking quickly in the same direction. I followed to make sure she was alright, but I kept my distance when I noticed Mary Beth nervously pacing outside of the ladies room, waiting for the woman to come out."

Luckily, the pub was quiet that night, and Sam was able to give Jenny his undivided attention.

"And… and…" Sam said, motioning with his right hand for her to keep talking.

Jenny took another sip from her glass, before continuing.

"When the woman came out of the ladies room, Mary Beth walked up to her, and said, 'Mom? It's me, Mary Beth. Is it really you?' The woman started to shake her head, saying 'I'm sorry pumpkin, I'm not your…' The moment she said that, Mary Beth cried, 'It is you! You always called me 'Pumpkin.' At that, they both started crying, as they began hugging each other. The next session was about to start, so I went back into the conference room. Minutes later, Mary Beth and her mother returned, quietly gathered their things and left."

"Did Mary Beth say anything to you?" Sam asked.

"She just excused herself, whispering that something came up, and that she had to leave."

"Wow. Isn't this interesting?" Sam said. "Apparently there is life after death. This piece of information could come in handy. Is there anything else?"

"Well, during the lunch break," Jenny continued, "I spoke to the man who had been sitting next to the woman. I explained that she looked familiar to me, but I couldn't remember her name. Without blinking an eye, he answered, 'Betsy Myers.' He then added that she had mentioned working as a bookkeeper at the Catholic Church in Sanford. I told him that's where I remembered her from and thanked him for his help."

"You are smart and beautiful," "Sam" said, adding, "And I owe you a nice dinner for passing along this useful information. Look… I'm off in twenty minutes. Let me go home, grab a quick shower, then I'll pick you up at your place. I'll take you to my favorite Italian Restaurant up in Wells. Does that sound good to you?"

"That sounds like fun. See you around seven, then?" she asked.

"Great! I'll be there Jenny."

They may call him "Sam" after the owner of Cheers, but watching Jenny walk out of the pub, made him feel more like Woody!

* * * * *

Like many Italian restaurants, the dining area was dark and cozy, with intimate booths lit by candlelight. Despite the darkness, Jenny's figure made a few heads turn, as she breezed by in her bright yellow sundress. Sam's ego got a boost from a few of the other male patrons, some of whom gave him a 'thumbs up'.

"Do you trust me?" he asked her, referring to the menu.

"Of course," she replied. "I love Italian. Order whatever you think I'd like."

Sam was pleased. The dinner was going quite well. She was laughing at all of his jokes, and enjoying his company. He could feel her sandaled foot brush up against his leg under the table.

As usual, the *Frutti di Mare* at Verano's was outstanding. Jenny thoroughly enjoyed her Chicken Parmesan, even though she was unable to finish the generous portion. "Sam" had selected the perfect wine for each of their meals, knowing that the proper pairing adds an extra element of enjoyment to any meal. She was surprised when he ordered a Bollini Merlot for her.

"I thought one always drank white wine with chicken?" she asked.

"A red wine, like a Merlot, is better when having pasta with tomato sauce," he explained.

For himself, "Sam" selected a glass of Le Bruniche Chardonnay.

"Where did you learn so much about wine pairings?" Jenny asked.

"I know what you're thinking," "Sam" said, laughing, "It's not like my customers are looking to find the proper wine to pair with their Buffalo wings or nachos!"

The wine was beginning to have an effect on Jenny, to "Sam's" delight.

She giggled. "I didn't mean it to sound like that. I was just curious. There seems to be more about you than meets the eye."

"It's nothing really. I simply read a lot." "Sam" explained. "The bar gets a complimentary subscription to *Wine & Dine Magazine*."

After dinner, "Sam" and Jenny drove to a nearby beach and watched the full moon rise over the ocean. They started kissing on the beach, but everything else happened at her place.

Leaving her apartment the next morning, "Sam" smiled and thought, *the proper wine pairing certainly does add an extra element of enjoyment to a meal.* While the sex with Jenny was great, "Sam" now had other thoughts on his mind that made him smile. It was time to put his plan in motion. A plan to make some easy money, and all he had to do was play his cards right. But first, he would need to do a little research, and aimed his car toward Sanford.

* * * * *

"Sam" was alone. The lanes were dark and quiet. He walked over to the seldom-used payphone near the restrooms, searched his pockets for the number he found on the Internet, dropped in a few coins and dialed. After a few rings, they answered.

"Hello?"

"I know who you are," he said, deepening his voice. "If you don't want me to tell anyone, you'll have to pay me to keep quiet. Think about it. I'll call back tomorrow."

* * * * *

Think about it. I'll call back tomorrow. That's all he said before the line went dead. *Who was he?* The voice was not familiar, and it did not sound as though he were trying to disguise it. *Who knew?* She nervously walked back to the living room, dropping herself into a club chair like a ten-pound sack of potatoes, searching her mind for possibilities.

That was yesterday. Today, Betsy jumped every time the telephone rang. She hardly received calls at home, but for some reason just because she was waiting for his call, every charity and telemarketer picked today to contact her.

At approximately 6:20 p.m., the same time as the day before, the telephone rang. It was the same voice.

"Hello, Elizabeth," he said, using her given name. "See, I do know who you are. Now listen to me. If you want to keep me quiet and prevent me from divulging your little secret to your family, it's going to cost you. I want cash every week. Not a large amount. Let's just say, you'll have me on retainer."

"But… I'm not a wealthy woman. I don't have any money," she replied. "There is no way I could pay you each week."

"Ah, but you do have access to money. You can pay me on *Mondays*, if you catch my drift."

"Mondays? I don't understand."

"Elizabeth… I'm surprised. Someone shrewd enough to disappear… for what… twenty-five years? And, you can't think of a way to get me money on Mondays?? Think of it as a 'second collection."

"Oh no. No, no. I couldn't steal money from the church."

"But you're the bookkeeper. A simple error turns a nine into a six, and suddenly there is three hundred dollars no one knows about. Think about it. I'll call you tomorrow, same time."

She walked back to her chair, sat, and once again searched her mind for possibilities of who it could be, and what she would say when he called her again tomorrow.

He was right. She did have a secret. Something she had done twenty-five years ago. It was easy to remember when it all began, because someone she knew reminded her of the fact, every time she saw her. She could only imagine how this would affect her family if they ever learned the truth.

Chapter 5

Detective Sergeant Warren Wilson quickly hung up his desk phone and grabbed his suit jacket as he headed for the door. He had just received a call from the hospital, causing him to jump into his cruiser and speed off. When he arrived, the doctor met him at the nurse's station.

"Is she well enough to talk, Doc?"

"She might be able to answer a few questions, but please take it easy," replied Dr. Robert Cartier.

"I only have two questions for her," he said, counting off with two fingers, "What's her name, and how'd she end up on the beach?"

The sergeant walked into the room behind the doctor, who gave her a quick check. Looking over the doctor's shoulder, Wilson saw her closed eyes and badly bruised face.

"Hello young lady. Can you hear me?" asked Doctor Cartier.

The young woman barely nodded her head, her eyes still closed.

"Are you able to talk?"

Her eyes opened slightly, and she opened her mouth attempting to speak, but nothing came out.

"May I ask her a question now?" the sergeant asked, looking over at the doctor who nodded, and stepped aside.

"Miss. I'm Detective Sergeant Wilson. Do you know your name? You just need to move your head, yes or no."

The patient opened her eyes again and nodded.

Can you tell me who you are?"

Again, her eyes opened, and swallowing hard, she tried to speak. "A... ME," she whispered, closing her eyes again.

"Amy... can you tell us your last name?" Wilson asked, trying to get another answer from her.

This time, Amy did not respond. "She's still very weak," the doctor explained. "Give her more time."

"Okay Doc. You have my number. By the way, I'm going to have my partner, Officer Marc Rousseau, come by to take her fingerprints. We may be able to identify her if she is military, or a government employee of some type."

"Fine, the doctor replied. But, when Officer Rousseau arrives, please have the nurses page me before he does anything. I would like to be present."

"Will do, Doc! Remember... call me with any update, and should she wake up again, notify the officer standing outside her door."

The doctor seemed reluctant, but agreed to comply. Walking back to his cruiser, Wilson made two calls from his cellphone. The first was to headquarters. He instructed Rousseau to first check missing persons for any women named Amy. Second, he told Rousseau to get her fingerprints, and run them through the system. The second call was to Anne.

"Mrs. Burke. It's Sergeant Wilson. The young woman woke up long enough for us to get a first name. Her name is Amy. That's all we know."

"When do you think we can see her?" Anne asked.

"I'm not sure. She's still too weak for visitors, and you're not a friend or a family member. I'll have to check with the doctor. Perhaps in a few days."

"Good. I can't help but think about her, I feel the need to talk to her. Thank you, Sergeant."

"Kevin!" Anne called out to her husband, who was watching "his" Chicago White Sox play "Annie's" Red Sox on TV. "Her name is Amy!"

Kevin muted the television and asked, "What was that?"

"Jane Doe's first name is Amy. Sergeant Wilson just called. He was able to briefly see her, and she was able to whisper her first name."

"Do you know any Amy's?" Kevin asked.

"No. You know I've never seen her before. But Sergeant Wilson said we might be able see her when she gains more strength."

* * * * *

When he returned to the station, Wilson met with Captain Peter Rudman, and Harbor Point's police Chief Sam Austin, to review the 'Jane Doe' case.

"What do you have so far, Warren?" asked the Chief.

"I just came back from meeting Dr. Cartier at County Hospital. Our Jane Doe is still recovering, and she seems to be going in and out of consciousness right now. The doctor said that's normal with the trauma she apparently sustained. I was able to ask if she knew her name before she blanked out again. She said her name was Amy. I've got Rousseau checking the missing person's database for any young women named Amy, Amelia, or other possible variations of the name."

"Good idea on the variations," Captain Rudman said, "That's my niece's name, but she spells it A-I-M-E-E."

"Thanks Cap. I'll let Marc know. By the way, Marc was wondering if we should post her photo to social media sites. He thinks it might help identify her."

"These young guys want to use social media to solve everything these days," the Chief said with a chuckle. "They're not interested in wearing out the soles of their shoes to investigate as we did before the Internet!"

The Chief looked at Wilson and asked, "What do you think, Warren?"

Glancing at his captain first, Warren replied, "I think we should hold off on releasing a photo. First of all, her face is rather bruised, and she sustained some cuts as well. Second, this is not like the Boston Marathon Bombing case, where they needed to ID the possible suspects PDQ. And finally, it's not like she's holding anything back. She told us her first name, and I'm sure she'll speak with me soon."

"I agree with your assessment on this one, Warren," the Chief said. "Live by the media… die by the media! Let's keep this one to ourselves for the moment. We don't exactly have the manpower to investigate every freaking 'Twitter' we'd get on MyFace anyway."

Rudman and Wilson nodded in agreement, each holding back a smile at the Chief's mention of MyFace. Apparently the sixty-five year-old chief liked to think he had a handle on social media, but never seemed to use the proper terminology, which caused a few chuckles within the department whenever he tried to do so.

"Do we have an officer standing outside her hospital room?" asked the Captain.

"Yes. The doctor has orders to let the officer know when she is coherent as well. He has instructions to ask her last name when she wakes up again."

"Excellent. Have you tried running her fingerprints through AFIS?" asked the Chief, referring to the Automated Fingerprint Identification System.

"Marc is heading to the hospital as we speak to do just that," Warren replied.

"Sounds like we're doing everything we can on this one, gentlemen. Keep up the good work," the Chief said standing, signaling the end to the meeting.

"Yes sir," the two junior officers replied, before leaving his office.

* * * * *

Callers to local radio talk shows kept the airwaves busy with speculation of who Harbor Point's 'Jane Doe' was, how she got on the rocks, and where she came from. On television, the story of the mysterious patient whispering her first name led the day's 5 p.m. news broadcast. B-roll taped earlier in the day from the beach near the Burke's summerhouse covered the screen, as the newscaster quoted un-named hospital sources, as stating 'Jane Doe' whispered 'A-ME' when asked by police if she knew her name.

Sergeant Wilson kept an eye on the television mounted high in the corner of the squad room. When he saw this piece of information on the news, he was pissed. *So much for HIPAA laws and medical privacy,* he thought. "Unnamed hospital sources, my ass. The only other person in the room when I interviewed Amy was Doctor Cartier," he said under his breath.

* * * * *

Sitting quietly in her apartment, Elizabeth was also watching the evening news. Not only did she have an idea who A-ME was, she recognized the stretch of Harbor Point Beach now on the TV screen. The only thing she didn't know was what her daughter was doing there! Unfortunately, circumstances did not allow her to contact the hospital to verify her thoughts. She simply turned off the TV and began to finger her rosary beads in prayer.

As she prayed, she asked for forgiveness for the sins of her past. Behind closed eyes, images of the life she once had flashed across her mind.

A few days before, she had seen Anne and Kevin as well as the police sergeant on the news. The sergeant, standing in front of the police station, gave the standard, police-issue 'non-response,' while Anne and Kevin answered the reporter's questions from the deck overlooking the beach. Neither had said much, but she sensed they knew more than they reported.

Anne had become a lovely, intelligent young woman, and had apparently found herself a good, loving husband, and handsome too. She had read the couple's engagement announcement in the *Portland Press*

Herald, and had cut the article from the paper. She hadn't shown the clipping to her daughter, Aimee. Why should she? Aimee did not know Anne or Kevin, and her mother's interest in the couple would have only raised more questions. Aimee Myers had been asking many questions of her mother lately; questions that her mother, Elizabeth Myers apparently didn't want to answer, responding only with questions of her own, such as, "Why do you want to know about that?" or "I told you all about your father when you were younger. He was a good man who died in the car accident the day you were born."

Young Aimee thought it strange that all of her friends had extended families of aunts and uncles, cousins, grandparents and siblings. As a child and later as a teenager, Aimee had accepted her mother's answers, only wishing she had known her father and other members of her mother's family. It wasn't until recently; when she spied her mother crying while looking at a scrapbook of old photos and newspaper clippings did she begin to wonder what her mother was hiding.

* * * * *

Elizabeth gently moved her Bible aside, allowing enough space to remove the scrapbook from her nightstand. The time worn album contained old photographs and newspaper clippings of her earlier life, duplicates of the originals she carefully assembled as she planned her disappearance. Over the past seven years, however, she had been able to add recent photos and clippings she came across in the local papers.

Sitting in the Canadian Rocker in her bedroom, Elizabeth touched the fading photos and yellowing newsprint in the scrapbook, feeding her memories of a secret life that began a little more than a quarter century ago.

Now in tears, Betsy remembered how her once happy marriage had become stale. Her husband began spending more and more time at work, leaving her at home with her two young daughters. He was doing everything he could to get his next promotion, a slot that would put him on track to someday be base commander, or even better, Air Guard Commander. She remembered how he would always say, "I'm doing this for you and the girls," whenever she would ask why he was working another weekend, or flying yet another mission. She would then give him a kiss goodbye, and tell him to come back safely.

Ironically, it was his ambition that had attracted her to him. His father had retired as a full colonel, and Mac was driven to do the same or better, by becoming a "one-star" general. Now Elizabeth understood why her late mother-in-law became an alcoholic.

Like many stay-at-home moms of the day, Elizabeth began to live her life vicariously through the characters of a TV soap opera. The secrecy, drama, and adultery, happening in the make-believe village of Lakeview between 3:00 and 4:00 p.m., Monday through Friday, captured Betsy's imagination.

That summer, when her husband introduced her to a colleague, she felt like the young nurse in her story, meeting the tall and handsome Doctor Williams. The attraction was instant, and she sensed the feelings were mutual. Unbelievably, he showed up later that week when her husband was away, her daughter was in school, and the baby was sleeping. Although the excitement of it all rekindled her spirit, it lasted only a few weeks. Twelve years of Catholic School instills enough guilt to last a lifetime, and as she sat through Sunday Mass with her family, she knew the affair could not continue. The following day, Betsy called to tell him it was over. He took it hard, but he understood. Unfortunately, she learned several weeks later that her life would soon mirror that of one of the characters in her story. She was pregnant, and ashamed.

Chapter 6

The next morning, Wilson sat at his desk shuffling papers. He was not satisfied with just knowing the young woman's first name. Searches of national missing person databases had not provided any leads. In fact, no one reported anyone named Amy 'missing' in the last 90 days. He moved a stack of reports needing his signature, and noticed the small evidence bag holding the locket the paramedics had removed from Amy when they treated her on the beach. He put on latex gloves and unsealed the bag, removing the slightly damaged locket. Grains of moist beach sand still covered the heart-shaped piece of jewelry, making opening the locket with his large fingers difficult, so he reached into his desk drawer for his letter opener.

Carefully, Wilson pried open the locket hoping to find an inscription or a photo that would help him fully identify Amy. When he opened the locket, he saw what appeared to be Amy's high school photo. As he glanced at the photo on the right, he saw a face he hadn't seen in nearly twenty-five years. He closed his eyes, and hung his head for what seemed like an hour.

Wilson picked up the phone and dialed the phone number he had written in his notebook earlier in the week. The phone rang several times before being answered.

"Hello, this is Doctor Cartier."

"Doc… Sergeant Wilson here… how's our patient this morning?"

"She is resting comfortably," he replied. "We're seeing some improvement."

"Can I stop by to see her? Do you think she'll be responsive to further questioning?

"She's been more coherent, so you may be able learn more about her situation today."

"Great. I'll be there within the hour."

Wilson quickly signed the pile of reports on his desk. Just as he was preparing to leave, Officer Rousseau poked his head in the office saying, "Sarge. I've got some information for you. First, I ran Amy's fingerprints through AFIS. We got a hit. Apparently she is a schoolteacher in Sanford. Her name is indeed Amy, but she spells it, A-I-M-E-E."

"Just like the captain's niece then," responded Wilson.

"Exactly," Rousseau said adding, "Her last name is Myers. We also heard from a man combing the beach near the rocks by the McDonald's home with his metal detector. He found this wallet and turned it in. Apparently this guardian angel coin hidden inside it set off his equipment."

Wilson grabbed the wallet from Rousseau's hand. "Does it belong to whom I think it does?" he asked.

"Yes. The ID matches the information from AFIS. Her driver's license lists her residence as 245 Mill Street, Sanford. Would you like me to get a phone number for that residence and contact someone?" asked Rousseau.

"No, I can take care of that, Marc," Wilson said to the officer, "I was just heading to the hospital to see her now. Thanks."

"Oh, and another thing, Sarge," Rousseau added, "Now that we know her name, it appears we have her vehicle in the impound lot. It was towed for parking longer than the posted time limit along the beach wall on Seaside Boulevard."

"Good work, Marc. Thanks."

* * * * *

The doctor was waiting for Sergeant Wilson at the nurse's station. "Hello, Sergeant. She's awake."

"Excellent. We located her wallet and her vehicle earlier today. Her name is Aimee Myers. This time I need to speak to her alone. I'll let you know if I need you. By the way doctor, I don't want to hear about any unnamed hospital sources leaking information to the media. Let the police department make any announcements about this case. Am I clear?"

Sergeant Wilson entered the private room, leaving Doctor Cartier by the nurses' station, somewhat embarrassed. Aimee was lying in the bed with her head raised. The doctor was right. She looked much better. She still had cuts and some bruising, but overall, she appeared to be better. The resemblance to Anne Burke was amazing, and he was starting to have an idea why.

"Hello, Aimee. I'm Sergeant Wilson of the Harbor Point Police Department. Do you remember me from the other day?"

She nodded. "Yes, Sergeant, I do. I guess I wasn't in any condition to speak with you though."

Wilson smiled and said, "Well, at least you were able to give us your first name, Miss Myers."

"How do you know my last name, then?" she asked.

"Your fingerprints. We also heard from a beach prospector who found your wallet with his metal detector, not far from where we found you. Apparently the 'guardian angel coin' inside set it off."

"I guess it does work!" she said with a smile. My mother gave it to me. She works at a church."

"Is this your mother?" Wilson asked holding up the locket.

"Oh my God! I didn't notice my locket was missing. My mom gave me that, too. I'm so glad you found it."

"Miss Myers," Wilson began, getting back on track. "What do you remember from that day? I mean, do you remember how you ended up on the rocks?"

* * * * *

"Can you believe it, Anne?" Kevin began, as they ate their breakfast. "Our honeymoon is almost over. We only have a few days left."

"What do you mean the 'honeymoon is almost over'?" she asked teasingly. "Is my 'Prince Charming' planning to turn back into a frog at midnight? If that's the case, I better take you to Harbor Point Light today, as I promised."

"Sounds like a plan. How 'bout we pack a picnic lunch, Mrs. Burke?" Kevin asked.

"A picnic? You're being pretty romantic for a guy who just said, 'the honeymoon is over!'" Anne teased again.

They finished breakfast, showered, dressed and walked up the street to a trolley stop. The Harbor Point Trolley Company provided inexpensive bus transportation throughout the Harbor Point area, with several stops at The Point, Harbor Point Beach, The Village, and hourly trips to Harbor Point Light State Park.

With picnic basket in hand, they boarded the trolley for the 15-minute ride to the lighthouse. On beautiful days like today, trolley drivers rolled up the clear vinyl covering the windows, giving passengers an open car experience. Anne chose a seat near the rear of the car and Kevin slid into the seat next to her. He placed the picnic basket by his feet, and draped his left arm around Anne's shoulder.

The trolley route traveled along Oceanside Drive, passing Harbor Point Creamery & General Store, The Lobster Trap Restaurant, Ocean Sands Beach, and several large private homes and summer rentals. People on their front porches and on the sidewalk waved to the trolley passengers as they passed by. After making several stops to pick up or discharge passengers, the driver turned the trolley, christened "Mollie," onto Lighthouse Road for the final mile of the trip. As they arrived at Harbor Point Light, the driver thanked his passengers for riding the trolley, reminding them the trolley departed Harbor Point Light at 20 minutes past each hour. Anne and Kevin stepped off the trolley and walked toward the footbridge, which connected the mainland to the small island on which the lighthouse stood.

Inside, Kevin and Anne joined a tour led by a volunteer docent who recounted the history of the light.

"Harbor Point Light is one of the oldest lighthouses in Maine," he began, his voice filled with false enthusiasm. "Built in 1879, a series of lighthouse keepers kept the light for nearly one hundred years, living in the adjoining keeper's house. During the Blizzard of '78, strong northeasterly winds and pounding surf destroyed the original house and the footbridge. Luckily, the lighthouse provided shelter for the 3-man station team, until the U.S. Coast Guard helicopter rescued them from the island several days later. That spring, the Coast Guard automated the light, which meant keepers were no longer necessary. Members of the Harbor Point Historical Society raised the necessary funds to rebuild a replica of the 1879 house. In 1982, the Society opened the replica keeper's house as a museum dedicated to the history of the lighthouse service in the United States. As part of the project, the town and the state developed the adjoining land as a state park with great views of the ocean and surrounding area."

After the tour, Kevin and Anne found a lovely shaded area with a view of The Point, and The Ocean House. They spread out a blanket and began to enjoy their lunch. Several minutes later, a couple walked over to where Kevin and Anne were sitting. They had been looking at them throughout the tour.

"Are you the couple who found that girl on the beach?" the woman asked.

"Um, yes we are," Kevin, said trying to swallow a bite of sandwich as he answered.

"We saw you on TV the other night," the woman began, speaking a mile a minute. "I noticed you on the trolley, and I said to my husband, Earl, here, 'There are those people who found that girl on the beach.' We just had to talk to you and ask if you know how that poor young girl is doing."

Anne answered this time, "We really don't know more than what they are reporting on TV. The police are investigating, but they are not keeping us updated."

The couple seemed to want to keep talking and kept asking questions about the incident, while Kevin and Anne tried to eat. Realizing they were not going to be able to enjoy the rest of their lunch and their visit to the lighthouse, Kevin said to Anne, "Honey, don't forget we have that appointment, and it's almost time to catch the trolley back to town."

"Oh, my, you're right," Anne said, looking surprised at the time. Looking at the other couple, Anne said, "We really need to get going," as they put things back into the picnic basket.

They said "good-bye" to the couple, and quickly walked to the trolley stop.

"Do you think we're ever going to enjoy a quiet lunch in Harbor Point again?" Kevin asked as they boarded the trolley.

"My God, they didn't stop talking!" Anne said.

"What do you mean, '*they* didn't stop talking?'" Kevin asked laughing, "*Earl* didn't say a word the entire time!"

Instead of returning home, Anne suggested they stop by The Point to visit the shops they hadn't gotten to earlier in the week. As they walked down the street, Anne noticed people kept looking at them.

"This is getting creepy," she said.

* * * * *

Sergeant Wilson listened intently, as Aimee recounted on how she ended up on the rocks that morning.

"A few weeks ago, the door to my mother's bedroom was slightly ajar. As I was walking by, I noticed she was looking at some sort of scrapbook I'd never seen before. I could see she was crying, so I knocked and asked if she was okay. She quickly closed the book, saying she was just reading a sad story, before going to bed."

"Did you eventually ask her about the scrapbook?" Wilson asked.

"No. After Mom left for work the next morning, I went into her room to look for the scrapbook, and some answers. It didn't take me long to find it in her nightstand drawer, hidden under her Bible, and the photo album she kept of our years in Boise."

"What was in the scrapbook?" Wilson asked, urging her to continue.

"It was filled with photos and newspaper clippings of people I've never met before in my life. I remember stopping at one photo and staring. It was apparently my mother's wedding picture. She looked so young and beautiful in her gown. Based on the date written on the back of the photo, Mom was eighteen years old when she got married. I assume the handsome man in the photo was my father. He was wearing a military uniform and was tall, fit, and looked very much in love with my mother."

"Do you know what happened to your father, Aimee?"

"Mom told me he died in a car accident. Apparently a car ran a red light slamming into the driver's side of my father's car. My father died at the scene, but my mother was taken to the hospital. She was in bad shape - unconscious - so the doctors delivered me, two weeks before her due date."

Wilson slowly shook his head letting out a low whistle.

"Before I knew it," she continued, "it was late afternoon. I had completely lost track of time, spending the entire day reading about a family I knew nothing about, but apparently, my mother did. Were these people part of her family… my family? There was one photo of my mother, her husband, a teenaged girl, and a baby girl. If they were family, why was my mother hiding from these people? I began to wonder if these girls were my sisters. If my father died, what happened to these two girls?"

As Sergeant Wilson listened, he occasionally jotted things in his notebook. Aimee explained that based on information and pictures she saw in the scrapbook; the people lived in a cottage at Harbor Point Beach.

"I thought if I took a walk or a jog along that stretch of beach early in the morning, I might pass the house and maybe run into the people I read about in Mom's book." With a slight shrug of her shoulders, she added, "I guess I hoped we would strike up a conversation, and I might get to know them."

"Sounds like something from a movie, Miss Myers," Wilson added during a slight pause in the conversation.

"Sergeant, you have no idea how many times I've headed for that beach in the past month, only to chicken out!"

"But it sounds like you finally got up your nerve," Wilson replied. "Now please tell me, how did you end up injured on the rocks?"

"I remember walking along and seeing the cottage beyond the breakwater. The tide was coming in, and breaking hard against the rocks. The only way to get to the other side of the beach was to go through the rocks. I remember thinking to myself that the rocks were awfully slippery, when a large wave came in and knocked me off my feet. As I started to get back up, another wave broke. The last thing I can remember is slipping and falling on the rocks."

"So you're saying you ended up unconscious, cut, and bruised, because you slipped on the rocks?

"Yes. The tide was very strong. I believe it was a full moon earlier this week," she replied.

"What is your mother's name, Aimee?"

"Betsy Myers."

An hour had passed, when Doctor Cartier poked his head into the room. He reminded Sergeant Wilson that while Aimee was awake and alert, she was still recuperating and needed her rest.

"All right Doctor. We're just finishing up," he said, turning to face Aimee. "Aimee, I'll contact your mother to let her know where you are. Okay?"

Aimee nodded, as Wilson walked toward the door. He suddenly stopped, turned and "pulled a Lt. Columbo."

"Ah. Excuse me, Miss Myers… one more thing. No one reported you missing. Not even your mother. You've been in the hospital for several days. Why wouldn't your mother report you missing?"

"Sergeant," Aimee began coyly, "I *am* twenty-five years old. I may share an apartment with my mother, but I don't *always* sleep at home."

Chapter 7

Betsy sat in her apartment anxiously watching the evening news. Expecting the phone to ring at any moment, but hoping it would not, she continually shifted her gaze from the TV screen to the telephone sitting on the table next to her chair. It was his usual time to call. Would he call again tonight as he had promised? She hoped he would decide to drop his attempt to blackmail her - encouraging her to take money from the parish's weekly collection. She absolutely would not do that. Who was he? How did he find out?

At exactly 6:20, the phone began to ring. The caller ID screen simply read "PRIVATE NUMBER," but she knew who was calling. She picked up the phone, but said nothing. Instead, she heard his voice.

"What's the matter, Betsy? Did you forget how to answer a telephone?"

"No… no, I didn't. Y-you just did not give me time to say 'hello,' is all," she replied.

"You sound scared, Betsy. Are you scared? Worried? Does it bother you that someone might tell your family that you're alive and well, and living in Sanford?"

"My family knows where I am," she replied, hoping to trip him up.

"C'mon Betsy. That's not going to work, 'cause, I know you're full of shit. The truth is, only your oldest daughter knows of your whereabouts. What's her name? Oh yeah… Mary Beth. And she won't tell anyone. Hell, for the first time, she has something her sister doesn't. You!"

Betsy started to cry. He knew too many details. How did he know?

"So Betsy… what's it going to be, huh? Money in my pocket… or do I call 'Good ole' Dick McDonald, the police, and the insurance company?

"Okay… okay. I'll give you money, but you leave my family alone."

"Smart move, Elizabeth. I'll call you at noon on Monday, with the details on how our little transaction is going to go down.

* * * * *

Wilson left the hospital and headed home to make the call to Aimee's mother. He had made many similar calls to give unsuspecting parents bad news about their children, however, this particular call would be difficult for another reason, which is why he wanted to do it from home.

Referring to his notebook, he called the number provided by Officer Rousseau.

Still sitting by the phone, Betsy answered on the first ring. "I told you I would do it, now stop calling me," Betsy said angrily.

"Elizabeth? It's Warren Wilson. I'm calling about your daughter Aimee."

"Oh, I'm so sorry for answering the phone like that. I've been getting harassed by a telemarketer," she said lying. "I saw you on the news, Warren. I figured you would eventually find out and contact me. How is she? Is Aimee okay?"

"She's fine… resting comfortably. The doctor said he would be releasing her in a few days."

"Oh, thank God. I've been absolutely miserable about this, considering the circumstances."

Wilson paused, and then asked, "Elizabeth… is she… mine?"

"No, Warren. Aimee is not your daughter. She's Mac's child."

"You do realize she has many questions, Elizabeth."

"I imagine you do, too."

"That's an understatement. Where do want to begin?"

"Warren, I'd rather explain it all in person, if you don't mind. Can you meet me at the Turnpike Diner in an hour?"

"Sure. I know where it is. I'll be there, Elizabeth."

"Please… I go by Betsy now."

"Okay Betsy. I'll see you in an hour."

Betsy slowly placed the phone into its base as she sat composing her thoughts. After twenty-five years of hiding, she wondered what her future now had in store. Because of Aimee's actions, she would finally have to come clean. Wilson knew who she was, and where she was. She no longer had a choice. She had to come out of hiding. What exactly would she tell Warren? And how much would she tell him? More importantly, what would happen when her husband found out she was still alive?

It suddenly dawned on Betsy that the situation with her mystery caller had changed in her favor. By coming out of hiding, he no longer had anything with which to blackmail her.

* * * * *

The Turnpike Diner was located on State Route 109, halfway between Harbor Point and Sanford. Although it appeared to be a typical roadside diner, its menu consisted of up-scaled versions of traditional diner fare. The restaurant was always busy, but its appearance on the Food Channel's hit show, "Would You Like Fries With That?" and its energetic host Chef Rick Tarantino, definitely put the Turnpike Diner on the map. It was now a planned destination for many of the show's fans visiting southern Maine. The increased interest generated even more media attention, and soon the walls of a recently added dining room were filled with autographed photos of celebrities taken when they visited the diner.

Wilson arrived with a few minutes to spare. He walked in and spotted her seated in a booth away from the windows, near the back of the original dining area. Her once shoulder-length black hair was now shorter and light gray in color. Wilson walked past the counter motioning to the server to bring him a cup of coffee. Approaching her table, he smiled, and sat down. After exchanging pleasantries, lying to each other about how they hadn't changed, Betsy took a cleansing breath and began to talk. Wilson did not hear the first few words she said, though. The truth was Elizabeth, he really needed to remember to call her Betsy, really hadn't changed. He still found her as beautiful as the day Mac had introduced him to her twenty-six years ago.

The arrival of his cup of coffee brought Wilson back to the present. He thanked the server, after she asked Betsy if she wanted her cup 'warmed up.'

"You were saying…" Wilson said, coaxing Betsy to continue, as he stirred crème into his coffee.

"I was so ashamed about our affair," she whispered. "Especially when I found out I was pregnant. I thought it might be yours, but I wasn't sure. It still could have been Mac's. I was ashamed and confused. I certainly couldn't hide it, and being Catholic, having an abortion was out of the question. One afternoon, I was watching my favorite soap opera on TV. Do you remember *Shadows of the Night*?"

Warren, still looking at her face, nodded once that he did.

"Well, one of the characters was in a situation similar to mine," Betsy continued. "She had a somewhat unhappy marriage, three young children, and she had an affair with her husband's friend. I remember how she just left one day. She vanished – disappeared, became someone else. That night I tossed and turned and didn't sleep a wink. For an entire week, I thought about how I could make myself disappear. I considered where I would go, and how I would support the baby and me. Finally, when Mac left for the base that Wednesday morning, I made my decision. After Mary Beth left for school, I prepared a bag for myself and diaper bag for Anne. I dropped her off with the neighbor, then came back to leave the notes for Mac and Mary Beth.

Wilson started to ask a question, but Betsy raised her hand stopping him saying, "Please let me finish."

He smiled, said "Okay," and took another sip of his coffee.

"I had saved up a tidy sum from the household budget over the years. When Anne got a little older, I had planned to surprise the family with a vacation to Disney World. Instead, I decided to use that money for my escape. I left my car in the grocery store parking lot and called a cab to bring me to the train station. I took the train to Logan Airport and bought a one-way plane ticket to Idaho. I figured no one would ever think of looking for me in Boise. Many people were moving to Boise at that time, so I did not raise any suspicions. I rented an apartment and got a part-time job at an Albertsons grocery store. When co-workers asked about the father of my baby, I told them her father had died in car accident shortly before she was born. I've kept to that story for the past twenty-five years."

Betsy stopped to take a sip of coffee, giving Wilson an opening.

"Betsy, how long have you been back on the east coast?"

"About seven years ago, Aimee and I moved to Concord, New Hampshire after she graduated from high school. Aimee's best friend applied to Plymouth State University, and I convinced Aimee to apply there as well. I remembered Plymouth had a great education department, and they both wanted to be teachers. I explained to Aimee that I'd be happy to move to New Hampshire, allowing her to take advantage of the lower in-state resident tuition costs. Although she lived on campus, Aimee liked the fact she was just a quick forty-five minute drive from home, rather than being six-hours away by plane. Living nearby also allowed me to see Anne graduate from Northeastern. I also sat in the back of St. James on her wedding day. She looked beautiful."

"Why did you never contact them when they were young?"

"I was too scared and ashamed. I had had an affair, abandoned my family, and was raising a daughter and sister they knew nothing about."

"What are you going to do now, Betsy? Aimee has pretty much figured it out, and Anne is wondering why this young woman, found near her home looks so much like her. Anne told me she has a strange feeling about Aimee. Betsy, someone needs to tell all three of your daughters the truth."

Betsy looked away and said, "I only need to explain it to two of them."

"What?" Wilson asked, rocking back in his seat with his eyes opening wide.

"What are you saying?"

"Mary Beth already knows about me and Aimee."

Wilson closed his eyes, pinching the bridge of his nose as he slowly shook his head.

"We ran into each other at a seminar for bookkeepers at the New England Center. She spotted me first and then found me during a break. She looked at me, glanced at my nametag and said, 'Mom, it's Mary Beth. Is it really you?' She had found me; I couldn't hide or lie to her at that point. It was an uncomfortable reunion, but we hugged each other and started crying. We left the seminar and found a coffee shop in Durham, where I explained everything to her just as I'm doing to you today."

"Why didn't you tell everyone else then?"

Betsy could no longer hold back the tears, and they began to flow freely down her cheeks, streaking her eye makeup.

"I don't know. I was so afraid. I made Mary Beth promise not to tell anyone about me. We've only spoken on the phone a few times since. That's how I knew about Anne's wedding. What should I do now, Warren?"

"The truth needs to come out, Betsy. As an officer of the law, I cannot keep this a secret. And of course, Mac, Anne, and Aimee deserve to know the truth. It will hurt, and there will be anger and tears. But, there will also be relief, healing and eventually, happiness too."

Betsy dabbed her eyes dry with the remnants of her napkin. "Can you take me to see Aimee?"

"Are you sure you don't want to wait until she's released from the hospital?"

"Yes, I'm sure. I want to get everything out in the open. I'm tired of hiding. There's one more thing. Someone else seems to know who I am. He has been calling me, blackmailing me, threatening to expose me if I don't pay him to keep quiet."

"Do you have any idea who he might be?" Warren asked.

"No. I've always been extremely careful. He called me 'Elizabeth.' I have not used that name in twenty-five years."

"So it has to be someone who knew you back then," Wilson said, thinking aloud. "What has he told you to do?"

"He said he'll call me at noon on Monday to make arrangements for the first payment."

"Betsy, I really don't think you have anything to worry about now. You just told me you're going to tell your family everything you've just told me. This scumbag no longer has anything over you. Next time he calls, tell him what you've done."

"I hoped you'd say that. Should I be afraid that he might try to do something else to hurt me or Aimee, now that he can't get money from me?"

"I've got a buddy at the Sanford PD. His name is "Buzz" Wilkinson. He's a detective. I'll give him a call, explain the situation and ask him to give you a call."

"That would be great, Warren," Betsy said, looking somewhat relieved.

"Don't worry, Betsy," Wilson said, placing his right hand over hers. "If that guy threatens you or Aimee in any way I'm sure Buzz will want you to call him right away. If he's not available, you can always call me. Alright?"

Chapter 8

Anne was alone at the beach house for the first time since before her wedding. She found herself with an abundance of nervous energy preventing her from concentrating on anything for more than a few seconds. Picking up the latest issue of *People* magazine, she tried reading an article, but quickly lost interest. She tried the TV, using her thumb to rapidly click through dozens of channels. Finding nothing of interest, she turned off the TV.

She jumped to her feet and began to pace the floor. After her third lap around the small cottage, she stopped at the open sliding door, gazing out at the rocks where they had found Aimee.

Anne knew the source of this nervous energy had nothing to do with Kevin having to unexpectedly go to his uncle's pharmacy for a meeting. Uncle Liam had called that morning, asking Kevin to stop by the drug store at 1 p.m. He had been working side-by-side with his uncle since graduating from Northeastern's School of Pharmacy. Anne hated to admit it, but the events of the past week bothered her, and they continued to gnaw at her subconscious.

What is it about this young girl? Why does she look so much like me? Anne thought. Then, remembering she had not heard from the police, she grabbed her iPhone, and selected Sergeant Wilson's number from her list of recent calls. After several rings, an automated voice mailbox system answered with instructions to leave a message.

"Sergeant Wilson. This is Anne Burke. I'm just calling to see if I… well if Kevin and I could meet Aimee anytime soon. Please let us know. Thank you. Good bye Sergeant."

She hung up and quickly selected another number. After two rings, a young female voice answered, "Hello."

"Hi, Sally. Is your Mom home?"

"Hey Auntie Anne… hold on, I'll get her."

Over the phone, Anne could hear her niece cover the phone with her hand, before she yelled, "Mom, Auntie Anne is on the phone." Seconds later, Mary Beth answered.

"Hi, Anne, what's up? How's your honeymoon going?"

"It's great, but Kevin had to go to a meeting with his uncle, so I'm here by myself."

"What's the matter? Are you lonely already?

"After a long pause, Anne said, "No. I keep thinking about Aimee."

"The young girl?"

"Yeah, the police said her name's Aimee, and I just can't stop thinking about her."

"Anne… we talked about this. I know it must be weird to find someone unconscious near our beach house, but you're a nurse. You see injured people all the time. Why does this one bother you so much?"

"Finding her is not what's bugging me. It's the fact she looks so much like me that's got me wondering who she is!"

After another long pause Anne softly asked, "Mary Beth, do you ever wonder what happened to Mom?"

"Ah… we're back to that Lifetime Channel movie. Annie, it's been twenty-five years…"

"I know. I know. You and Dad have moved on. Even though I was just a toddler and hardly knew her, I just can't seem to get over the fact she left us. I've always wondered why," Anne said with a sniffle. "When I was younger, I thought maybe she left because of me. I remember breaking that model air refueling tanker Dad kept on his desk. Mom took the blame, saying it fell onto the floor and broke when she was dusting his study. They had a big fight that night. She left a few weeks after that."

"Oh, honey… you have to stop blaming yourself for Mom leaving. Do you really think she actually left because Dad yelled at her about one of his stupid model airplanes? Anne, I think the stress of everything going on in your life – the wedding, the honeymoon, and finding the young girl on our beach, is really starting to wear on you. Maybe you should ask Kevin to bring home some pills to relax you. There's got to be some perks for being married to a pharmacist!"

"Mary Beth… there's more. I think I keeping seeing Mom."

"What? Where do you think you've seen Mom?"

"I thought I saw her at my high school graduation and again when I graduated from Northeastern."

"Lemmie guess. I bet you think you saw her at your wedding, too?

"You saw her too, didn't you?"

"Anne," Mary Beth said annoyed, "You need to get a grip! Have a glass of wine, throw *Sleepless in Seattle* into the DVD player, and relax."

"I've already tried watching TV. I can't seem to sit still. I'm just a ball of nervous energy."

"Go for a run then," Mary Beth suggested. "That's what you used to do to clear your head."

"That's a good idea! Kevin won't be home for a bit. Maybe I will."

"Good. Are you feeling better now, Sis?

"Not really. Maybe I will after the run!"

Changing the subject, Anne asked, "What are you up to this weekend? Are you and the kids coming to the beach house?"

"We might if Dad is going. I guess it really depends on the weather. If we do, we'll see you Saturday morning. At least you and Kevin can have one more night of honeymoon to yourselves! Bye, Annie."

* * * * *

Mary Beth didn't even take the time to hang up the receiver. She pressed 'end call', and quickly dialed a number she knew by heart, but had only called a few times.

Damn, she thought. *Why isn't she home? Where is she? I wish she had given me her cell phone number. I wonder if she went to County Hospital to see Aimee?*

* * * * *

This is too easy, he thought. *I bet I can play this from both sides,* as he picked up the phone and dialed.

"Hello?"

"Your mother is alive and well and living in the area. I know where she is."

"Who is this?" demanded Anne.

"Who I am is not important, but what I know is. I know where your mother is living. Pay me five thousand dollars, and you can have your mommy back."

"Who are you, and how do you know about my mother?"

"Look sis… put the money in locker number 11 at the Peter Pan Bus terminal on Monday, and you'll be talking to your mother by Monday night."

He hung up the phone and smiled.

Anne hit the speed dial number for Kevin's cell phone. It went right to his voice mail. She then tried Sergeant Wilson's number. He was unavailable, too. She thought of calling her father, but he usually flew commuter flights from Portsmouth to Boston to Cape Cod on Fridays, and probably wouldn't be answering his phone either.

Mary Beth's right, thought Anne as she hung up the phone. *I need to get over Mom leaving us; I need to move on too. Her leaving wasn't my fault. Mary Beth and Dad managed to put the twenty-five year-old memories to rest. I have to as well.*

Anne felt a slight smile cross her face as she remembered her sister's 'prescription' for the afternoon. She walked into the kitchen and took a bottle of White Zinfandel from the fridge. She poured herself a glass of the wine, cut a few slices of Monterrey Jack and shook a few wheat crackers from the box onto a plate next to the cheese.

Padding into the living room, Anne searched their selection of DVDs for *Sleepless in Seattle.* Finding it, she put it into the player and settled in for the afternoon with her wine and cheese. As the opening credits rolled, Anne thought to herself, *what was Mary Beth thinking? In the movie, Jonah's mother dies, and his dad, played by Tom Hanks moves to Seattle to start over, to get over the wife he'd lost, to move on.*

"How is this movie supposed to make me feel better?" Anne asked herself aloud. Mary Beth was right about one thing. The stress from months of preparing for the wedding and wishing her mother had been there to share the happy experience was wearing on her. Finding an unconscious young woman on the beach that looked as though she could have been her kid sister was almost enough to put her over the edge. Anne's thoughts turned to Aimee once again. Aimee... *Who are you? Why were you on the rocks? Is it just a coincidence that you look like me, or is there something else?*

Anne downed the rest of the wine in one swallow, deciding in the process to go to County Hospital to see Aimee herself. She had asked Sergeant Wilson for permission to see her several times already, and he never responded. *Screw him, I'm going anyway. I need to resolve my 'need to know' about her,* she thought as she grabbed her purse and car keys on the way out the door.

* * * * *

Kevin arrived at the drug store and walked into the back office he shared with his Uncle Liam. Expecting only to find his uncle, he was surprised to see their attorney and accountant there as well.

"Hey, guys! Uncle Liam, what's going on?" Kevin asked as he shook hands with everyone present. "I thought you said you just needed to go over a few things with me before you went on your vacation. Why are Ted and Jerry here?" he asked referring to their legal and financial advisors.

"Have a seat, my boy," Uncle Liam said, pointing to desk chair he had just vacated, opting for comfort of a small couch.

"Kevin," Uncle Liam began, "the truth is I am not a well man. I'd hoped to work by your side for the next four years, but my doctors tell me I shouldn't. So I've asked Ted to draw up the paperwork to transfer majority ownership of the drug store to you now."

"What do you mean you're not a well man? What's the matter?"

"Doc Gagnon says I have a serious heart condition and don't need the additional stress of worrying about the business. That's why I'm turning it over to you now rather than later. Don't worry. You're ready. You're a 'pharmD' after all," he said, referring to the fact that pharmacists now graduate with a 'Doctor of Pharmacy' degree.

"Ted… Jerry… explain the transfer papers to Kevin, and let's get everything signed today."

Although the advisors reviewed the paperwork explaining the details, Kevin realized he was focusing more on his uncle's condition than on the financial and legalese he was hearing. Now that he knew the situation, he realized the darkened circles under his uncle's eyes, and recently acquired mannerisms had been masking worry and physical discomfort.

An hour into the meeting, Liam Burke squeezed his eyes shut tight in pain, while grabbing his left arm with his right hand.

Immediately, Kevin and the advisors reacted. Ted called 9-1-1, Jerry went to wait for the EMT's outside, and Kevin tried to make the old man comfortable on the office couch.

After calling 9-1-1, the lawyer looked at Kevin and quietly said while motioning with his head towards the couch, "He's already signed the paperwork. You may want to sign it too, before you go to the hospital with him."

Twenty minutes later, paramedics had Liam loaded onto a stretcher and into the ambulance headed to County Hospital, its flashing lights and blaring siren announcing the urgency of the trip. Kevin followed behind in his car trying to keep up with the speeding ambulance.

* * * * *

Mac McDonald had taken the day off, and was surprised when he arrived at the beach house earlier than expected and did not see at least one car in the driveway. He knew both his daughter and son-in-law had driven their cars to Harbor Point Beach before the wedding, so to see both cars missing made him a little wary. He let himself in the side door and immediately saw the note written in Anne's handwriting on the kitchen counter. The note simply read, Kevin – gone to hospital.

Gone to the hospital? Why? Mac thought. Anne was not going back to work for another four days. Mac picked up the phone and punched in Mary Beth's number.

"Hello."

"Hi Sally, it's Grandpa. Is your mom home?"

"No Grandpa, she left saying she had to go to the hospital."

"Did she say why?

"No. She just said she had to go to the hospital."

Mac wondered what was going on. His son-in-law was not home, and his two daughters were going to the hospital for some unknown reason.

* * * * *

"Call – beach - house," Kevin said aloud, activating the Bluetooth option in his car. Instantly, the car's speakers came to life with the sound of the phone ringing. *"C'mon Annie, pick up,"* he said to himself.

After several rings, Mac picked up the phone. "Hello."

"Mac? Hi, it's Kevin. Can you put Annie on the phone?

"She's not home Kevin. I just got here myself. I found a note she left for you on the kitchen counter. It says she's gone to County Hospital. It almost reminded me of…" his voice trailed off but then he quickly, said, "Never mind. I just called Mary Beth's house and Sally said her mom left for the hospital too. She didn't know why."

"Mac, I'm on the way to the hospital, too. Uncle Liam collapsed during a meeting at the store. I'm tailing the ambulance up Route 1 now. Can you get over to the hospital, too? I have no idea why Annie and Mary Beth are heading to the hospital, but someone needs to be with my uncle, and I can't be in two places at once."

"Sure, I can be there in 10 minutes. I'll meet you in the ER lobby," he said grabbing his car keys from the counter. "See you in a few."

Kevin began to ponder why both Annie and her sister were heading to the hospital. Did either of them hurt themselves? No. If that were the case, Sally would have known why her mother went to the hospital. It had to be something else. What could have happened? It suddenly dawned on him as he passed *Flowers by Amy*, the shop where Annie had selected their wedding floral arrangements. *Aimee*, he thought. *She must be going to the hospital to see Aimee. Sergeant Wilson probably finally called to say it was okay for Annie to come down to see Aimee.*

* * * * *

Wilson and Betsy arrived at County Hospital and entered by the main visitors' lobby.

"She's on the fourth floor," Wilson said as they approached the bank of elevators.

"How do I look? Is my make-up okay?" Betsy asked. "I probably should freshen up before seeing her. Are the rest rooms nearby?"

Wilson looked at her, remembering how he felt about her during their brief affair all those years ago, he smiled at her and replied, "Betsy, you look fine."

"I should visit the ladies' room anyway," she said, noticing the sign adjacent to the elevators.

"Fine, I'll wait for you here."

Just as the door closed behind her, Wilson turned, glancing back towards the lobby and saw Anne walking through the large revolving doors. *Oh great,* he thought. *This is not good.* Betsy was ready to explain everything to Aimee, but he was not sure if she was quite ready to re-enter Annie's life too. Would she lose the nerve to go through with this if she knew Anne was in the building?

Luckily, for Wilson, Anne did not know Aimee's room number so she had to inquire at the patient information desk, and there were several people in line.

Timing is everything and the elevator doors parted just as Betsy was leaving the ladies' room. Wilson instinctively reached to hold the doors open with his right hand as he motioned for Betsy to hurry with his left.

Entering the elevator, he pushed the 'fourth floor' button and the 'close doors' button in quick succession.

"Are you in a hurry?" Betsy asked, noticing Wilson's apparent rush.

"Force of habit," he replied rather matter-of-factly, with a sheepish grin.

The elevator quickly rose to the fourth floor without a stop in between.

"She's in room 420," he said, pointing towards the left as they exited the elevator.

"Does Aimee know I'm coming?" Betsy asked.

"How could she? I didn't know you would come until an hour ago.

Wilson would have liked to prep Aimee beforehand, but with Anne in the building, he didn't have that luxury.

"Would you like me in the room while you talk with Aimee?"

"No. I think I need the 'mother-daughter' time. It might be especially awkward especially since you are involved. Do you mind waiting outside in the hall?"

"I don't mind at all. I understand." *Another bit of luck*, he thought. He could wait outside the door and intercept Anne when she arrived.

"Room 420 is two doors down on the right," he told Betsy as he stopped by the nurse's station. "I need to check in with the nurse manager."

Wilson watched as Betsy tentatively approached the door to her daughter's hospital room. Once she was inside, he turned to check in with the nurse on duty, only to see her speaking to another young woman. His ears perked when he heard her question to the nurse.

"Hi. I'm looking for room 420."

"Are you a member of the family?" the nurse asked.

"Yes. I'm… um… her older sister," she replied.

The nurse quickly glanced over at Sergeant Wilson, who was now looking at the woman standing nearby.

"Excuse me, ma'am," he asked. "Are you Mary Beth McDonald?"

"Yes, but my last name is Mason, now. And you are?"

"Sergeant Warren Wilson of the Harbor Point Beach Police department," he answered with his right hand extended for a handshake."

"Oh. Sergeant Wilson. Yes. My sister Anne mentioned your name. I remember meeting you at the air base when I was a kid."

"Yeah, that was a long time ago," he replied with a smile. Looking over to the nurse, Wilson said, "Thanks, Karen. I'll show Ms. Mason the way."

Wilson cupped Mary Beth's left elbow gently guiding her away from the nurse's station.

"Your mother is in with Aimee right now. She is telling her everything."

Mary Beth's hand rose to cover her mouth as a look of surprise came to her face and tears to her eyes. Experience told Wilson what she was thinking, so he answered her questions before she could form the words.

"The only thing we found with Aimee was a locket she was wearing. She was not carrying any other forms of identification when we found her. A beach prospector found her wallet in the sand later that day. The paramedics removed the locket from around her neck when they stabilized her on the beach. As part of my investigation to identify Aimee, I pried open the locket revealing two faces, one of those being a picture of your mother. I recognized her immediately and contacted her based on information we found in Aimee's wallet. She told me everything that happened twenty-five years ago and since then, including how you ran into her at that conference in Durham."

"Does Anne know any of it yet?" Mary Beth asked, brushing the tears from her eyes.

"No, not yet, but your mom is tired of hiding and plans to tell Anne and your father as soon as Aimee is discharged from the hospital."

The "ding" announcing the arrival of an elevator, caught Mary Beth and Wilson's attention and they both looked in the direction of the elevator bank.

As she exited the elevator, Anne looked in both directions to get her bearings, performing a perfect "double-take" as she noticed Mary Beth standing with Wilson in a small waiting area.

"What are you doing here Mary Beth?" Anne asked as she walked in their direction. "Sergeant… why are you talking with my sister? Is this about Aimee?

"I located Aimee's mother and brought her to the hospital to see Aimee. She is in with her now. They have a *few* things to discuss. It may take a while. Do you two want to wait and speak with Aimee afterward? I'm assuming that's why you're both here."

"It is Sergeant," Anne replied. "You never returned my calls about seeing Aimee, so I decided to come to the hospital, myself. Kevin had a meeting this afternoon, leaving me home alone with just my thoughts about everything that has happened lately. There is something about all of this that keeps bugging me, which is why I'm here. I still don't understand why you're here Mary Beth, and why you are speaking with the Sergeant?"

"One of my neighbors called me after I spoke with you this morning, asking if I could give her a ride to the hospital. She wanted to visit a relative who is a patient. While waiting for her, I recognized Sergeant Wilson from the TV reports, and I remembered you said that he knew Dad and how we had met him when we were kids. I had just introduced myself, when you arrived."

Wilson could hardly keep the corners of his mouth from forming a grin, as he listened to a thinly disguised version of the truth.

* * * * *

Not quite knowing what to expect, Betsy slowly pushed open the door to Aimee's room. As she entered, Betsy peered around the edge of the door, seeing her daughter's gaze turn toward the door.

"Mom!" Aimee said happily.

"Yes, Sweetie, it's me," Betsy replied stepping into the room. I came to see how you were doing. Sergeant Wilson contacted me and told me you were here."

"I guess I have some explaining to do, huh?" Aimee asked, spreading her arms in reference to the room.

"No, Sweetie, I think I'm the one who needs to do the explaining. Sergeant Wilson told me why you were on that stretch of beach. I know you have many questions, and it's time you know the truth."

Aimee saw the tears begin to run down her mother's cheeks. "Mom… it's alright. I love you no matter what you're going to tell me.

Betsy noticed the tears well up in Aimee's eyes as well, and they hugged each other tightly for several minutes. The embrace ended with both women laughing and wiping their eyes.

"Silly emotional women," laughed Aimee, shaking her head.

"Silly emotional women," Betsy repeated in agreement, laughing, before stopping to clear her throat. Holding her daughter's two hands, Betsy began.

"Aimee, I'm not sure where to start, but I think you've figured out that there is a part of my past that I haven't been honest and open about with you. You have two older sisters, a father, and a …

"New brother-in-law?" Aimee asked, finishing her mother's sentence.

"Yes. Anne and Kevin Burke, the people who found you on the rocks, are your sister and brother-in-law. Your other sister's name is Mary Beth. She has two children, named Sally and Drew."

"Wow. Not only do I get a dad, two sisters and a brother-in-law, I get a niece and nephew too? Cool!" Aimee said, taking it all in.

"Mary Beth knows about you… about us."

"So I guess my father didn't die in a car accident?" Aimee asked.

"No, your father is still very much alive and lives in Portsmouth," Betsy replied, quickly adding, "There really was a car accident the day you were born though. It happened in Boise. I had just left work, and was driving down East Parkcenter Boulevard, when a car ran a red light, broadsiding me. As I told you many times, I was in really bad shape, unconscious really, when they brought me in. The head nurse told me the EMTs who responded to the accident were very concerned that I might not make it, so they delivered you in the ambulance on the way to the hospital, just in case."

The tears began to flow freely again for both women - tears of joy for Aimee, tears of relief for Betsy. She now felt as if the weight of the world had been lifted from her shoulders that afternoon, thanks to her earlier talk with Wilson, and now, as she opened up to Aimee. The two most difficult hurdles were still to come though – Anne and Mac.

Chapter 9

Kevin followed the ambulance through the 'ambulance only' access into the hospital's campus, but once inside took a quick left into the parking area. He noticed Annie's blue 2003 Toyota Camry as he came around the corner looking for an open parking spot. As luck would have it, a beat-up Oldsmobile Ciera was pulling out of a spot several spaces from Annie's car. Kevin eased in to the space and quickly ran inside to check on his uncle.

Mac was already in the Emergency department's waiting lounge. He stood and walked over as Kevin breezed through the automatic doors.

"How is he? What happened?" Mac asked.

"He had just finished telling me he was turning over the business to me earlier than planned, due to his poor health, when he collapsed with chest pains.

The two men approached the woman at the admission desk.

"Hi," Kevin began, "my uncle was just brought here by the ambulance. Can you tell me where he is?"

The look on the woman's face said it all. She didn't need to ask the question.

"His name is Liam Burke. B-U-R-K-E."

"He is your uncle?" she asked, not looking up, as she searched and pecked with two fingers across the computer's keyboard.

"Yes. We're also business partners. We own a neighborhood drug store. We're pharmacists," Kevin said, offering more information than she truly needed.

"He's in exam room 3." Motioning to the waiting area, she said, "You can wait in the lounge while the doctors examine him. I'll let them know you're here. Someone will be out to inform you of his condition as soon as possible."

Before Kevin could ask another question, she was already talking to the family standing behind them. She hadn't even given Kevin an opportunity to ask another question. Without even saying, "next!" she had effectively pushed them aside.

Walking slowly back to the waiting area, Mac gently patted his son-in-law on the back saying, "He'll be okay, Kevin. Don't you worry."

"I know. I guess I'll just wait here until they tell me what's going on. I probably should call my dad to let him know Uncle Liam is in the hospital, huh?"

"Good idea," Mac answered. "In the meantime, I'll track down Anne to let her know you're here too. What's that girl's name you think she came to see?"

"Aimee… Aimee Myers.

"Got it. I'll be right back."

Mac gave Kevin a quick tap on the arm, turned and walked over to hospital directory. Locating the patient information desk on the map, he took a left and followed the red line on the floor to the main lobby.

The main lobby was light and airy, and reminded Mac of an airline terminal with all sorts of people going in different directions. To the left of the main entrance, the lobby featured a small gift shop, a florist, a Dunkin' Donuts, and a fast food sandwich shop called "Stat." There was even an ATM conveniently located nearby. *They've thought of everything*, Mac said to himself.

The young woman at the patient information desk was much better suited for customer service than the other woman, Mac thought, as he stood in line. She had a genuine smile, happy eyes, and handled the questions with professionalism and a certain amount of confidentiality. He noticed her ID badge. Her name was Stacey, and in bold letters across the bottom, it said, "Volunteer." *How nice*, he thought. *It was good to see young people volunteering at the hospital.* He wondered if they still called them 'candy stripers?

When his turn came, Stacey smiled, and politely asked Mac if she could help him.

"Yes. Can you tell me which room Aimee Myers is in?"

Following a flurry of keystrokes at the computer, Stacey told Mac that "that patient" was in room 420, and offered directions to the elevator that would bring him closest to that room. Unlike the woman at the ER, Stacey asked Mac if he had any other questions before she moved to the next person in line.

Leaving the desk, Mac got his bearings and headed in the direction of the elevators Stacey had pointed out. Pushing the 'up' call button, Mac waited for several minutes before an elevator opened for him. Mac stepped in joining a group of what appeared to be interns. Pressing the button for the fourth floor, Mac noticed the only other button lit was for the sixth floor, so he knew his stop would be next.

* * * * *

Wilson and Mary Beth kept to the story about the chance meeting, and filled the time with stories about Mac, the Guard, and their lives. After a while, Anne began to get impatient.

"What's taking her so long? I just want to say 'hello,' can't I just stick my head in the room to say 'hi'?"

Then looking at Mary Beth, she asked, "How long was your neighbor planning to visit with her relative? She seems to be MIA, too."

"My neighbor's sister just learned she has terminal cancer. I am sure they are comforting each other. I told her to take her time. I'm okay. Sally is home with Drew."

The elevator doors parted and Mac stepped out.

"Dad?"

"Mac?"

Anne had her back to the elevators, but upon hearing Mary Beth and Wilson, she turned, adding her own query at the sight of her father arriving on the fourth floor.

Mac immediately heard the familiar voices calling him. He looked to his left and started walking towards the small group with a somewhat quizzical look on his face. He knew Anne and Mary Beth were at the hospital, but what were they doing with his old friend Warren Wilson? Then he remembered Kevin saying Wilson was the detective in charge of the investigation. Perhaps he was the reason his daughters were here.

"Hi, Girls," Mac said, his eyes meeting Wilson's as he approached. Both Anne and Mary Beth met their father halfway each giving him a quick hug and peck on the cheek.

"Mac," Wilson said with a quick nod of his head while extending his hand toward Mac. "It's been a long time."

"It's been twenty-five years," Mac answered quickly, accepting Wilson's proffered hand.

The quick and exact response, made Wilson feel somewhat ill at ease. "It's been too long," he added.

Mac looked at his daughters, and then at Mac asking, "What's going on?"

Mary Beth replied, "We should ask you the same thing, Daddy. Why are you here?"

Suddenly remembering his mission, Mac looked at Anne.

"I came to find you. Kevin is downstairs in the ER with his Uncle Liam. Liam collapsed during their meeting, and the ambulance brought him here about ten…fifteen minutes ago. I answered the phone when Kevin called the beach house to let you know. When I told Kevin about your note, he asked me to meet him here."

"Oh my God," Anne said, her hands covering her mouth in shock. "Is Uncle Liam alright?"

"The docs are evaluating him now. Kevin is calling his Dad while he's waiting to hear about Liam's condition. You should go to him. I think he has other news for you, too."

Nodding her head, Anne began collecting her things. Mac gave Wilson a half-smile, shook his hand again saying, "Call me. We'll grab a beer at the Pease O Club and catch up."

"Sure, that would be great," he answered, returning Mac's firm handshake. In his mind, Wilson was beginning to thank God for this miracle. He knew Betsy had no idea this impromptu get together was happening in the hallway. Not knowing how things were going in Aimee's room, he did not want Betsy to feel ambushed should she suddenly come out of the room. It may be too soon for a family reunion, and the fourth floor of the hospital was definitely not the place to have it.

Down the hall, Aimee and Betsy had spent nearly ninety minutes discussing the past twenty-eight years, including her reasons for her leaving. In turn, Aimee explained how she ended up on the rocks, and in the hospital.

Suddenly, Betsy remembered that Wilson was still waiting in the hall. At least she hoped he was still there. He was her ride home!

Betsy excused herself and stepped out into hall to check in with Wilson. Luckily, she was in a hospital, because what she saw brought her to the floor.

* * * * *

Miracles happen every day at the hospital, but today was not that day for Wilson. Apparently, he had thanked God a little too soon for Mac's arrival to take Anne from the fourth floor.

As they both agreed to catch up over a beer, Wilson noticed Mac was no longer looking at him, but over his shoulder, towards Aimee's room. *Shit*, he thought, and closed his eyes.

"Elizabeth?" Mac asked when he saw Betsy leaving the room.

Hearing her father, Anne quickly turned around. Her eyes opened wide, and her jaw dropped. She pulled in a long breath through her mouth, before saying, "M-M- Mummy?" sounding like the little three-year old she was the last time she saw her mother.

Wilson and Mary Beth looked at each other, not knowing what to expect at this point.

Betsy had come through the door with a big smile on her face, but that smile turned to a look of shock as she heard her name, and her eyes saw who had said it. Her eyes darted to Mac, to Wilson, to Mary Beth, and then finally to Anne, who had turned and was quickly walking back to the little group.

It was too much for her. She hadn't expected it to happen this way - not here, not now. She was overwhelmed, and her mind's circuit breakers tripped. Betsy suddenly dropped to the floor like a ten-pound bag of Maine potatoes.

Immediately, nurses were at her side. A teen-aged visitor seeing what happened, absent-mindedly yelled, "Someone dial 9-1-1!"

Everyone in the hall stopped and looked at him.

"Whaaat?" he asked, before realizing how silly his statement was, considering they were in a hospital. Then, as if the light bulb finally turned on above his head, he said, "Oh ya... d'uh... I'm in a hospital. Sorry!" as he continued on his way.

The McDonald family gathered around their estranged mother and wife, with Wilson behind. A young doctor dressed in green hospital scrubs replaced the nurses at Betsy's side. Waving a packet of smelling salts under her nose, Betsy suddenly came to. She would be okay, the doctor proclaimed.

"She'll have a nasty bump on the back of her head, but she'll live," he said with a smile, helping her sit up as he looked up at the family.

Hearing the commotion outside her room, Aimee opened the door.

"Mom!" Aimee screamed, approaching her mother.

"Mom?" Mac and Anne asked in unison.

"How are you feeling?" the doctor asked Betsy? "Do you think you can stand?"

"I'm still a little lightheaded," she replied. "I'd prefer a chair."

"There's a nice chair in my room, Mom," Aimee said. "Doctor, can you help me get her into my room?"

"Elizabeth? Is it really you?" Mac finally asked, a tear rolling down his cheek.

She didn't look at him, but nodded as Aimee and the doctor helped her into the room and into the chair.

Chapter 10

So many things were now going through Anne's mind. Her mother appears from the room of the young woman she found lying unconscious on the rocks outside her house. That woman, who looked like her twin, even more so now that the swelling and bruises had faded, called her "Mom." Uncle Liam and Kevin are downstairs in the Emergency department, and… it suddenly dawned on her that Mary Beth had not been as surprised to see their mother or their "sister" as she and her father had been.

Similar thoughts crossed Mac's mind, except his centered around his old friend Warren Wilson. He obviously knew that Elizabeth was in that room, and that Aimee was her daughter. Why didn't he say anything? Why did he keep all of this information a secret? Twenty-five year old suspicions and thoughts returned from the corners of his memory. This was the first time he saw Aimee, and he couldn't help but see the resemblance to Anne. *Was Aimee 'a McDonald' or 'a Wilson?'* he thought?

Mac turned to Wilson, his mind still in 1983, when he was an Air Force captain and Wilson was a young sergeant, although they were actually about the same age.

"Sergeant! What the hell is going on here? Why wasn't I notified that my wife had returned?" his voice and anger increasing with each question.

"What do you know, and how long have you known about this? You have some explaining to do sergeant. I want answers, and I want them <u>now</u>," Mac said with authority and with emphasis on the word 'now.'

All eyes were on Wilson, from hospital staff, to Anne and Mary Beth, to visitors and curious patients who peered out from their rooms. Wilson, realizing he had an audience, knew how important it was for him to now react calmly and professionally. He held his hands up, shoulder height, with his palms facing Mac.

In calm, soothing voice, he replied, "Mister McDonald," adding a slight emphasis to the 'mister,' to snap Mac from his military stance. "Let's go to someplace more private where I can explain everything. Nurse, is there a conference room we can borrow?"

"Certainly," the head nurse replied, "there is one near my station."

"Thank you," Wilson said smiling at her. He then turned to Mary Beth and said, "Mary Beth, would you please tell your mother and sister that we'll be down the hall? I'd like you to join us too. We'll all come speak to your mother and Aimee in a few minutes."

Looking at Mac and Anne, Wilson extended his arm inviting them to lead the way to the conference room. Anne gave Mary Beth a stern look. She had some explaining to do too.

* * * * *

Doing as instructed, Mary Beth entered Aimee's room to explain what was happening.

Seeing her mother seated in the chair, Mary Beth asked, "How are you feeling, Mom?" before leaning over to give her a hug.

"About as well as could be expected under the circumstances. I see your father hasn't lost his temper. I heard the way he spoke to Sergeant Wilson."

Breaking the hug, but still holding her mother's shoulders, Mary Beth replied, "Actually, it's the first time I've heard him raise his voice like that in years."

Betsy sighed and said, "I guess he has a right to be upset. Hopefully Warren can calm him down a bit."

Mary Beth stood and looked at Aimee. She wanted to give her a hug too, but hesitated to make the first move.

"Hi, Mary Beth, I'm Aimee. I guess we're sisters," she said extending her arms as she stepped forward towards Mary Beth.

"Yes, we are," she said as the two women hugged each other tightly, tears freely flowing down their faces.

"Mary Beth, what's happening in the hall?" Betsy asked.

"Sergeant Wilson asked me to tell you that we will all be in to speak with you in a few minutes. He took Dad and Anne into a conference room to let them calm down and to explain a few things. I have to join them."

"It wasn't supposed to happen this way, you know."

"Yes, Mom. I know. I'm sure Sergeant Wilson will get Dad and Anne over the initial shock of seeing you rather unexpectedly. You can't really blame them for being upset. I don't know how I'm going to explain to them that I knew you've been around, though?"

"Mary Beth, just tell them the truth… that I made you promise you wouldn't. They are already upset at me. One more reason won't matter!"

"I have to go. I'll see you in a bit."

She bent to give her mother another hug, and whispered, "I love you," in her ear.

"Me, too, sweetheart… Me, too."

* * * * *

No one spoke on the way to the conference room. Wilson, Anne and Mac were each sorting things out in their heads. Even as they walked into the room, Wilson motioned to them to have a seat without saying it. The silence continued until Mary Beth joined them and sat down.

Wilson thought about standing, but changed his mind. He remained seated and began. "I'll be happy to answer your questions after I explain how these things played out."

Wilson took a deep, calming breath, slowly exhaling through his nose. He looked at each member of the McDonald family in the eye, and then said, "I began to piece everything together yesterday, when I opened the locket Aimee was wearing when we found her. I recognized Elizabeth's picture inside, and learned during an interview with Aimee, that the woman in the photo was her mother. Aimee said her mother's name was Elizabeth, but she preferred 'Betsy.' Her last name was Myers, and they had moved here from Boise, Idaho, when Aimee came east for college."

Mac quietly said, "Myers… that was her mother's maiden name."

Wilson continued. "I contacted Elizabeth and confirmed her identity as Aimee's mother. I met her in a restaurant in Sanford this morning, and she explained everything to me and agreed to tell Aimee. I was planning to contact all of you later today to set up a similar meeting where Elizabeth would explain the past twenty-five years to all of you. She's tired of hiding and wants to make peace with all of you."

Looking Mac squarely in the eyes, Wilson said, "I know you're first question. She's yours, Mac. Aimee is your daughter. Elizabeth and I did have a brief affair before she left, but, Aimee is your daughter."

A single tear ran down Mac's cheeks.

At the revelation of the affair, Anne and Mary Beth looked at each other. Even Mary Beth had not known about that part of the mystery.

"I know Elizabeth wants to tell you everything, and she will, but I wanted you to hear about the affair from me. It was my fault. It lasted only two weeks, and she broke it off. I'm sorry I ruined our friendship, Mac."

Once again, tears began to fall, this time like rain on the faces of Mac, Mary Beth and Anne. Wilson realized they needed time to process all of this information as a family, and he knew there was still more to come.

"Listen," he said, "it's getting late. The doctor is releasing Aimee tomorrow morning. Under the circumstances, I'm going to see if Elizabeth can spend the night in Aimee's room. I can bring both of them by the beach house in the morning if that is okay with you?"

Mac nodded his head, wiping his eyes with a handkerchief he pulled from his back pocket.

"Sergeant?" Anne asked.

"Yes, Anne."

"What was Aimee doing on the rocks?"

"She was in the dark about your mother's past as well. She had started putting some pieces together after finding a photo album filled with pictures and newspaper clippings. She was trying to learn more about the family in the pictures when she fell walking across the slippery rocks."

Now standing, Wilson reached for the doorknob and opened the door. "Stay here for a bit while I check on things, okay?"

Heading back to Aimee's room, Wilson saw a bewildered Kevin looking about.

"Mr. Burke!"

"Sergeant Wilson. Have you seen my wife and father-in-law?"

"Yes I have. They are right in there," motioning to the conference room.

"Look. You should know we just had a little excitement here."

"What happened?"

"In short, they saw Elizabeth."

"Annie's mom is here?"

"Yeah… and there's more. Aimee is your sister-in-law.

Wilson saw Kevin connect the dots in his head.

"Wow."

"By the way, how's your uncle?"

"He'll be alright. He's resting comfortably on the third floor."

"I'm glad," Wilson said. Motioning to the conference room, he added, "Why don't you join your family? I'll be right back."

* * * * *

Wilson knocked on the door before walking into Aimee's room.

"Are we okay in here?"

"Yes. Come in Sergeant," he heard Aimee reply.

"Well, that worked out nicely," Wilson said, shaking his head, pinching the bridge of his nose as though it would help relieve the headache he was getting.

"What happened in the other room? What did Mac and Anne say? What did you tell them?" Betsy asked in a flurry of questions.

"First of all," Wilson began holding out his thumb, as though he planned to count his responses. "I explained to them that I learned about your existence just recently, when I opened Aimee's locket and saw your picture."

The index finger extended as he said, "Two - I told them we met earlier today and that you explained everything to me. They know you're tired of hiding and want to tell them everything."

With three fingers now showing, he added, "I told them about the affair, that it was my fault, and that you broke it off after two weeks."

After a few seconds of silence, he added, no longer counting with his fingers, "I told Mac that Aimee is his daughter."

Aimee cleared her throat, furrowed her brow as she looked at her mother and said, "Uh… Mom. You didn't tell me about *that* part a few minutes ago?"

"I know. I'm still ashamed about it," she said looking apologetically at Wilson.

Not wanting to get into that discussion, Wilson interrupted with what he had come into the room to say.

"It's getting late, and emotions are understandably rather high right now. The doctor is releasing Aimee tomorrow. Considering what just happened in the hallway, Betsy, I'm going to ask if you can spend the night here in this room. I'm going to suggest to everyone that we meet at the beach house in Harbor Point tomorrow. Having these discussions is a private family matter. I think everyone would be more comfortable in a family setting. Are you okay with that?"

Betsy closed her eyes as she took a deep breath, exhaling slowly to compose herself.

Nodding she answered, "Yes. I guess that would be the best place for everyone concerned."

Betsy glanced in Aimee's direction, looking for agreement. Aimee responded by reaching over to give her mother a reassuring hug.

Wilson left mother and daughter in their room, in search of the nurse manager. Finding her at her desk, Wilson asked, "Is Aimee still being released in the morning?

"Yes, she is. The doctor just needs to sign the patient release form."

"Good. Would it be all right if her mother stays with her tonight, considering what happened in the hallway?"

Having witnessed the ordeal, the nurse responded with a nod, adding, "I'm pulling a double today, so I'll be here all night. I don't see a problem with it."

"Great. Thank you. I'll be by to pick them both up in the morning."

* * * * *

Wilson walked to the conference room to rejoin the other members of the McDonald family.

"How are we doing in here?" he asked as he strode through the conference room door.

Emotions in the room had settled a bit, however, he still sensed an underlying tension between Anne and Mary Beth.

"Here's what's going to happen," Wilson began. "Aimee is being released at 9 a.m. tomorrow morning. The nurse said she'll let Elizabeth stay the night, so I'll pick them both up here, and drive over to your place on the beach. Are you still okay with that plan?" he asked, looking at Mac.

"Yes," Mac replied with a sniffle, holding back his tears.

"Good. I'll see you all in the morning, around ten. I know it will be difficult, but try to get some rest tonight."

He shook everyone's hand before leaving, and added, "I hope your uncle gets well soon, Mr. Burke."

With that, he escorted them to the elevator. Kevin and Anne stopped on the third floor to check in on Uncle Liam before leaving. Wilson, Mac and Mary Beth rode the rest of the way down in silence. They shook hands again, and went their separate ways.

"Dad, are you going to be alright? I should go home to make supper for Sally and Drew. Do you want to join us?"

"No. I'll see you in the morning. I just need some time to myself. I'll grab something at the house later. Thanks anyway."

Mac leaned in to give his daughter a hug. Whispering in her ear, he said, "Mommy's back Sweetheart… Mommy's back."

Chapter 11

That night, sleep was impossible for everyone involved. In the hospital, Betsy lay awake staring at the ceiling, rehearsing in her mind what she would say to her husband and daughters. She thought about meeting her grandchildren and son-in-law for the first time. She wondered how the members of her family would accept her story and her reasons for leaving. Knowing Mac had never remarried, she wondered if he would be open to picking up where they left off. In a way, she fretted like a young schoolgirl before a first date. It had been twenty-five years since she last spoke to her husband, but she saw him at Anne's wedding, as she sat in the back pew, wearing a dark wig and glasses as a disguise. For a man of his age, he was still handsome, tall, and carried himself with an air of confidence. Seeing him walk Anne down the aisle reminded her of why she had fallen in love with him all those years before. He was quite a catch. *Why had she thrown all those years away?*

A few feet away, Aimee's mind was working overtime as well. She now had an instant family - her <u>real</u> family. She had prayed for this ever since she was a little girl, when she had envied her friends who had a father and siblings. She had long dreamt about how celebrating holidays like Thanksgiving and Christmas would be with a family. Aimee eventually fell asleep with a smile on her face.

Back at the beach house, the lights were on late into the night. In the master bedroom, Mac sat looking at an old photo album he remembered leaving in the back closet. In his mind, he, too, wondered what the future held for his marriage. *His marriage,* he thought. Wilson had said Elizabeth was tired of running and hiding. Did that mean she just wanted to make herself known? Or, might she be hoping to be a wife and mother again?

Two doors down, Anne and Kevin had many things to talk about. The day had started out rather routinely, but certainly ended as a day to remember. Kevin told Anne about his meeting with Uncle Liam, gaining ownership of the drug store, and his uncle's collapse.

The discussion then turned to Anne's day, her telephone conversation with Mary Beth, her decision to go to the hospital to see Aimee, and her surprise to see Mary Beth already there with Wilson. Finally, she recounted how her mother stepped out of Aimee's room shortly after her Dad showed up looking for her. Kevin listened intently as Anne described the events that led to her mother fainting in the hallway and the de-briefing with Wilson in the conference room.

Kevin could tell Anne was still upset, and he gave her a look that she knew was his way of asking, "Okay, what's really bothering you?"

"I am so mad at Mary Beth. Can you believe she has known about Mom for a while now and never said anything to us? She's kept this from Dad and me. How could she do this? You should have heard her on the phone this morning."

Using a sarcastic sounding voice, Annie vented more.

"Oh, Annie, you need to get over this. Annie, you need to move on. This is not some Lifetime Channel Movie where the long lost mother comes back!"

Back to her regular voice, Annie continued her rant. "Arrgggh! She said all this to me knowing that Mom was alive, living just a few towns over from us, and that Aimee was our sister! She even had the nerve to tell me to take something, have a glass of wine and watch *Sleepless in Seattle*."

Then poking Kevin in the shoulder, she said, "And get this," once again using the sarcastic voice, "she said there should be some benefit to being married to a pharmacist!"

Kevin suppressed a smile at that comment and thought the title of that night would be 'Sleepless in Harbor Point!'"

"Well… do you want something?" he asked.

"Kevin, I'm not in the mood!" she responded.

"Uh, I meant something to relax you."

"Yeah, right!"

"By the way, Anne, I really wouldn't recommend taking pills with wine. Just saying."

Wilson had things on his mind, too. Things the others probably hadn't thought about yet. The state of New Hampshire had legally declared Elizabeth Myers McDonald "dead" in 1990, seven years after her disappearance. Bringing her "back from the dead" would require some work no doubt. He imagined the insurance companies would have a field day over this one, too. Shaking his head, he thought, *only the lawyers are going to get rich on this one.* With that thought, he rolled over and tried to get some sleep.

Chapter 12

As expected, it was a "short night" for everyone. Shortly after 7 a.m., Doctor Cartier came in for one last check of Aimee's condition. Satisfied, he signed the patient release form and wished Aimee well.

Having heard about the previous afternoon's ordeal, he turned to Betsy, "How are you feeling this morning, Ms. Myers? I understand you fainted in the hallway yesterday. Would you like me to check your blood pressure?"

"No thank you, doctor. I'll be fine. I was just a little surprised at seeing my husband and daughters. I wasn't expecting them."

My husband, she thought. She hadn't used those words in so long. Again her thoughts from the previous night returned. *Would he take her back? Could they live together as a married couple again?* Living alone all these years, she had certainly gotten set in her ways. She imagined it was the same for him. Being a pilot, he was accustomed to having a set routine. She remembered he liked things neat, orderly, compartmentalized.

When the doctor left, Aimee quickly took a shower and put on the clothes Betsy had brought from home. She was anxious to get the day started.

Betsy showered and dressed, and they waited for Wilson to arrive.

At the beach house, Mac was up and out the door early. He left a note saying he was going to the grocery store to get some things for a continental breakfast. He always thought it was easier to discuss difficult things over food, and he figured Aimee and Elizabeth might not have had breakfast at the hospital. He ended the note with a request for Anne to make some coffee.

Mary Beth pulled in just as her father was leaving. They each stopped, rolling down their windows.

"Mornin' guys! I'm just going to pick up some breakfast for our guests. Can you make some coffee?"

He smiled, waved at his two grandchildren in the back seat, and drove off.

Breakfast for our guests? Mary Beth thought. Is that how he is thinking of them… as guests? Mary Beth's night had been short as well. She knew she also had explaining to do today, knowing very well that Anne was not going to let this pass. She might be happy about having Mom back today, but eventually, Mary Beth knew Anne would want some answers.

The door to Aimee's room was open when Wilson arrived at 9 a.m. as expected. He walked in to see both women ready and waiting to leave.

"Are we ready for this?"

"To be honest, I'll be glad when it's over, Warren," Betsy said.

"Understandable," he replied, then looking at Aimee, said, "Are you cleared for takeoff young lady?"

"Yes sir. Signed, sealed, and soon to be delivered."

They left the hospital, thanking the nurses as they passed. Wilson managed to get a parking spot close to the door, and helped Aimee and her mother into the back seat.

"Wow. This is nicer than the last police car I was in," Aimee said.

"When were you in the backseat of a police car, young lady?" asked Betsy.

"I have my secrets too, Mom!" she replied with a smile.

Small talk about the weather and the Red Sox filled the minutes of the short drive from the hospital.

Wilson parked in the street behind Mary Beth's minivan. Getting out, he opened the door for his two passengers.

"Thank you, Jeeves," Aimee said, with a big smile on her face.

"Aimee! Show some respect to Sergeant Wilson."

"Kids, these days!" he said shaking his head smiling.

Mac opened the door as the trio approached. Betsy couldn't help but notice Sally and Drew with their noses up against the picture window, getting their first look at their long-lost grandmother, and new young aunt. Aimee saw them, too. She winked and waved her fingers at them.

At the door, Mac shook Wilson's hand and using his military voice again, said "Good morning Sergeant."

"Good morning, Mr. McDonald."

With a sigh, Mac said, "Warren, this is silly. We're old friends, please, call me Mac."

In a softer, almost shy voice, he then looked passed Wilson at Aimee, smiled and said, "Hello, Aimee."

"Hello, Daddy," she said going in for a hug, which he accepted reluctantly at first, eventually putting his arms around her to return the hug.

Betsy stood at the door, watching her twenty-five-year-old daughter meet her father for the first time. She remembered the last time she walked through this door, she had just learned she was pregnant with Aimee and was contemplating her disappearance. Life is funny that way. It often seems to come back full circle, no matter how much you try to change its course.

Mary Beth and Anne stood a few feet behind their father, taking it all in, wiping tears from their eyes. Mary Beth looked to her mother for some sort of sign. A sign, that she was ready to do this; to re-enter her life, as a wife, mother and grandmother. Anne on the other hand, focused her attention on Aimee. This young woman, whom she last saw badly bruised and unconscious on the beach no more than 100 feet from where they stood now, had returned, not as a grateful stranger, but as a biological sister she never knew existed, and with her, their mother, who had disappeared so many years ago.

How will Dad react today? Anne kept asking herself since returning from the hospital. The initial shock, surprise and anger of seeing his estranged wife at the hospital had since evaporated. His actions this morning were rather cute and sweet, she thought. She smiled when she noticed he had tried on several different shirts, before deciding on the dark blue polo and khaki colored pants.

Running out to get items for a continental-style breakfast, figuring they would not have eaten breakfast before leaving the hospital was telling too, especially the carton of orange juice with 'no pulp'. Dad always bought 'all pulp.' She didn't know, but she was willing to bet that her mother didn't like pulp in her orange juice.

Everyone's attention now focused on Betsy and Mac. Here it was. That awkward, pivotal moment, thought Anne. *What would the moment be? Friendly, but formal - or welcoming and forgiving?* Betsy stepped forward, and Mac met her halfway. He looked her in the eye and said, "Welcome home, Elizabeth, we've missed you so much." He followed the comment with a long hug.

Once again, tears flowed freely on every member of the family. Finally, Mac said, "Everyone, please sit down. Help yourself to some breakfast. Are you hungry? Kevin, bring in the coffee from the kitchen."

On her way to the couch, Aimee introduced herself to Sally and Drew.

"You can just call me Aimee. Never mind that auntie stuff," she said to them with a quick wink and a hug. "We'll talk later!" Sally and Drew looked at each other and said, "Cool!"

They all sat down in the family room as Kevin poured the coffee.

Sitting on the edge of the sofa, holding a mug of coffee with both hands, Betsy looked at the floor. With eyes closed, she inhaled deeply, followed by a slow, deliberate exhale. Biting her lower lip, she looked up, and said, "Before I start, I want to apologize to each of you – Mac, Mary Beth, Annie, Aimee, Sally, Drew, and you, too, Kevin, for all of the hurt, worry, anger, and disappointment I have caused you to feel over the past twenty-five years."

She then looked directly at Anne, then at Mac. "I know you are both upset with Mary Beth for not telling you. Please do not blame or hold a grudge against her. I made her promise that she would not divulge my secret to you. We accidentally ran into each other at a seminar at UNH. She noticed me and came over. It was not my intention to make myself known to you then."

The other members of the McDonald family were quiet, giving their full attention to the wife and mother they had not seen in years.

"I was totally selfish in my reasons for leaving back then. I did not leave because of anything said or done to me. I wasn't happy with my life. I was depressed. I was discouraged, I felt ashamed. I felt trapped. I had had an affair I was not proud of, and I found myself pregnant. I needed help, but could not bring myself to admit it to you. As I explained to Sergeant Wilson yesterday, I got the whole idea from 'my story.'"

She sniffed, and gave out a chuckle of embarrassment, asking, "Remember 'my story' – 'The Shadows of the Night?'"

Mac nodded his head slowly, saying, "You never missed an episode. I remember you planned your day around that show."

"Yes. I was a bit obsessed. In my depressed state of mind, I used a storyline from the show to help plan my escape. I thought if I left everything in Exeter, my troubles would be left behind, too.

"What did you do? Where did you go, Mom?" asked Anne.

"I took the train to Boston, and then bought plane ticket at Logan Airport. I flew to Idaho and created a life in Boise. That's where Aimee was born.

"Is that the place that has the college with the blue turf football field?" Drew unexpectedly asked.

Both Betsy and Aimee smiled at his question.

"Yes, Drew. Boise State does have a blue football field. We lived not far from the campus."

"When I arrived in Boise, I began using my mother's maiden name, Myers, and I told people to call me 'Betsy' instead of Elizabeth. When people asked where my baby's father was, I told them he had recently died in a car accident and that I had moved to Boise to be away from all the memories of him."

"I found a job and made new friends. I did see a psychologist, but I stuck to my story, not mentioning my true past in New Hampshire. Eventually, with his help, I began to feel better about myself. Having to raise Aimee on my own actually helped. My mind focused on her well-being, and my job helped keep my mind off everything I left behind here. The holidays and your birthdays were tough to handle. More than once, I began to dial the phone to wish you a happy birthday, or Merry Christmas, but I would always hang up. I could not bring myself to reveal my whereabouts. Eventually, thanks to the Internet, I learned I had been declared dead, and I figured you guys had probably moved on with your lives. The last thing I wanted to do at that point was to return and wreak havoc on your lives once again."

Tears filled Betsy and her daughters' eyes again, and Kevin used the opportunity to "warm up" everyone's coffee.

Mac sat back in his chair, hiding his emotions. Throughout her twenty-five year absence, he had never really voiced his own feelings about his wife's disappearance to his family, other than words of comfort to his daughters, during those times when they missed their mom.

Wilson remained in the background, standing off to the side, leaning against the wall by the sliders, where this strange case had begun.

He occasionally turned to take in the view of the beach, imaging what it had been like for Anne to see Aimee's body on the rocks. His plan now was to keep quiet, to listen, and to keep the peace should things get out of hand. He was confident at this point that he wouldn't be needed in any official role or to serve as a mediator. He probably would not even need to bring Betsy and Aimee back to Sanford. At this point, he was quite sure they'd get home without any problem.

Mac's question to Betsy brought Wilson's attention back to the room though.

"Elizabeth… or would you prefer I call you Betsy now?" he asked. There was a hint of sarcasm in his voice, which prompted angry looks from all *three* of his daughters. Noticing their faces, he quickly apologized, saying, "I'm sorry. I didn't mean for it to sound that way. I… I always called you Elizabeth, but I can call you Betsy if you like that better."

"I've kind of gotten used to being called Betsy," she replied.

"Okay. So what brought you back to New England?"

"I saw an opportunity to get back here when Aimee was looking at colleges. Her best friend was looking at Plymouth State, so I convinced Aimee she should go there as well, by promising her I would move to New Hampshire, too, so she could get the resident tuition rate. After college, Aimee got a teaching position in Sanford, so I moved again. I got a job as church bookkeeper three years ago, and I've been there ever since."

"Where do you teach school?" Mac asked Aimee.

"I'm a first grade teacher at Springvale Elementary School. I love spending time with the kids. I think it's because I never had any siblings growing up."

"Well you do now," Mary Beth and Anne said, surprised at themselves for saying it in unison.

"I know," Aimee responded excitedly by coming to them for a group hug, as though they were kids again.

At that, Mac and Betsy looked at each other and smiled like the two proud parents they were.

When Aimee returned to her place on the couch next to her mother, she picked up the storyteller's role.

"A few weeks ago, I walked past Mom's room. Her door was barely open, but I could see that she was looking at a scrapbook of some kind and crying. I knocked and asked if she was okay. She quickly closed the book and said she was just reading a sad story, before going to bed. The next day, after she left for work, I looked through her nightstand for the scrapbook."

Before continuing, Aimee looked at her mother, "Sorry for snooping through your things, Mom."

"I looked through the scrapbook and found all sorts of old photos and newspaper clippings of people I didn't know. I began to piece together that the people in the album were close to my mother somehow. She never spoke about her family other than in generalities. I was the only kid in school who had never met her grandparents or father. Finding this scrapbook made me start wondering if I did have family members nearby. Mom had clippings about your graduations, wedding announcements, and a copy of feature article about you Dad, when you flew the first NH Air Guard tanker plane to refuel Air Force One over the Atlantic."

Sally and Drew looked at their grandfather with awe. "You never told us about that Grandpa," Sally said.

"Remind me the next time you're at my house. I have some pictures in my office and a letter from the President."

"No way…" an impressed Drew responded.

"Way," Mary Beth replied, proud of her father.

"So how did you end up on the rocks? Kevin asked.

"I started 'Google-ing' all of the names in the clippings – your names. Have you ever 'Google'd' your names? If not, you should. I read all kinds of things about this family and the disappearance of an Elizabeth McDonald. I began to get goose bumps. The similarities and the timeline were too much of a coincidence. I had to meet you. I thought if I walked on the beach, I might 'casually' run into you, and start talking with you. It sounds like a Lifetime Movie, doesn't it?"

The Lifetime Movie reference caused Anne and Mary Beth to glance at each other.

"I was trying to cross the breakwater. The rocks were rather slippery and when this huge wave came, it knocked me off my feet. I must have hit my head on the rocks, because the next thing I remember, I was in the hospital."

A knock on the front door, grabbed everyone's attention.

"Who could that be?" Mac wondered aloud.

Wilson suddenly became aware of activity happening on the beach, just as his cellphone began to ring.

"This is Sergeant Wilson," he said, answering his phone.

Wilson listened to the caller, waving his hand at Mac not to answer the front door.

"Okay, send a car here just in case," he told his caller before ending the call.

"Well, the media found out Aimee left the hospital and came here. They also found out about you Betsy. This is going to be breaking news all over the country, I'm afraid."

"How did they find out so fast?" asked Betsy.

"I'm thinking someone at the hospital leaked the story."

The house phone began to ring. Drew looked out the front window and saw several TV trucks setting up outside.

Wilson said, "I'll step outside and handle the first round of questions. I was going to mention this later, but Betsy's return has legal implications. You should contact your attorney. You may also ask him or her to serve as the family's spokesperson as well."

"Good idea," Mac said, taking out his cell phone, as he walked to where they kept the phone book."

Wilson opened the door to a crowd of reporters and a few curious neighbors. Immediately, questions showered Wilson from every direction.

"Why did he bring Aimee Myers back to the McDonald's home? Were the reports about her being the daughter of Mr. McDonald's estranged wife true? Was it also true that Mrs. McDonald was indeed alive and back in the area? Was she inside? How is the family handling the news?"

Wilson raised his arms to quiet the reporters as he began to supply rather broad answers to their questions. In a matter-of-fact way, he explained that Aimee Myers, the young woman found on the beach, was indeed, related to the family. That she was the daughter of Mr. McDonald and his wife Elizabeth, who had disappeared in 1983. He informed them that Mrs. McDonald was inside re-acquainting herself with the members of her family.

Ignoring the follow up questions thrown at him, Wilson concluded the impromptu press conference by saying, "Folks…This has been a traumatic and emotional time for the entire McDonald family. They are requesting their privacy for the time being, and I hope you will respect their request until they are ready to come forward. At such time, a spokesperson for the family will be happy to answer all of your questions."

To the police officer standing nearby, he said, "Officer, please escort these nice people to the property line."

Re-entering the home, he asked how things were in the house.

"Dad's on the phone with his lawyer right now. Sounds like he may be coming here within the hour," Anne replied.

"Betsy… Aimee…" Wilson began, "I have to go back to the station and close the case. Are you okay here? Do you want to go back home?"

"I think we'll be okay." Looking at Mac who was entering the room, she asked, "You don't mind if we stay a while, do you Mac?"

"Of course not, you're probably safer here," Mac replied. "You're with family. We can take you to Sanford later, if you'd like. Whatever you want."

"Thank you, Mac."

"Okay, then. I'll be heading back to the station. Let me know if you need anything. I'll be in touch. The officer will be outside for the remainder of his shift. I imagine once your attorney makes a statement on behalf of the family, they'll be satisfied for today at least. Oh, also I'll contact the

Sanford PD, to give them a heads-up too. The press might stalk your apartment there as well."

"Thank you, Warren," Betsy said.

Mac extended his hand and said, "Thank you, Warren."

Wilson gave the others a wave as he left the house.

* * * * *

Attorney David Greenville arrived forty-five minutes later. After learning the details, and conferring with his clients, it was time for him to speak to the press camped on the street outside. He began by repeating Wilson's earlier request for privacy on behalf of the family, telling reporters that while this is a happy moment for the family, there are obviously personal issues with which they are dealing. He promised them his office would release an official statement from the family in a few days.

Despite the promise of a statement, the reporters immediately began to toss questions in his direction.

"I don't have to remind you something like this does not occur every day. The family inside is reuniting with a loved one who voluntarily disappeared twenty-five years ago, and through a strange turn of events has made herself known to her family. That's all I have to say at this time."

Greenville returned to the house to inform his clients what was said, only to find them all in front of the television, listening to the reporters and news anchors opining about what was happening inside the McDonald home, and what would happen over the next days for the family.

They applauded as he entered the door. "Thank you, but believe me this will not die down until something else big happens to bounce you off the front pages, or until you all agree to do an on-camera interview. I'm expecting my office to be deluged with calls from the networks, movie producers, and authors, all wanting to tell your story."

Picking up his briefcase, Greenville said, "I should get back to the office to begin preparing the statement and look into any precedent for bringing Elizabeth McDonald "back to life."

With both Sergeant Wilson and Attorney Greenville now gone, the family spent the remainder of the afternoon asking and answering each other's questions. Everyone was playing 'catch-up,' attempting to fill in twenty-five years of lives spent apart.

Noticing the time, Kevin excused himself to check on Uncle Liam at the hospital.

Chapter 13

On most summer nights, Mac and his family would be relaxing with a glass of wine on the deck, enjoying the refreshing sea breeze, the surf breaking along the beach, and the aroma of something delicious on the grill. Unfortunately, with the press still camped out on the beach, the three McDonald sisters decided to go into the kitchen to prepare dinner. Mary Beth suggested to Sally that she and her brother go upstairs to play video games.

Looking at her parents, Mary Beth said, "You two need time to discuss things privately. Besides, we need to get to know our little sister!" she said with a wink.

Mac and Betsy laughed.

"It's almost as though they're kids again, Betsy."

Once their daughters had left the room, Betsy spoke.

"You've done a fine job raising the girls, Mac. Thank you. I'm sure it wasn't easy raising two girls without a mother around, not to mention the emotional baggage my leaving must have caused."

"Mary Beth did her best to fill your shoes as a mother to Annie. I don't know what I would have done without her. Looking back, I now realize how much I took her for granted. It's probably why she got married right out of high school. She spent so much time making sure Annie was okay, she didn't have time to concentrate on her own studies. Her poor grades denied her college entry after high school, and when Annie did so well in school, I think she resented Annie for her lot in life. They're okay now, but I sometimes think it still simmers underneath. It exposed itself when we learned Mary Beth knew you were around and didn't tell us."

"I know. That's why I told you this morning that I made Mary Beth promise to keep my existence a secret. She did try to get me to at least call you."

"So what happens now, Betsy? You started this story. How does it end?"

"I'd like to be back in your lives, Mac. I've missed so much already. I don't want to miss any more."

"I don't think that will be a problem. They are thrilled to have you back," he motioned toward the kitchen with his head.

"What about you? Betsy asked softly.

Mac paused, leaned forward in his chair, hands folded, with his arms resting against his thighs. In a voice, slightly louder than a whisper, he replied, "A day has not gone by, that I haven't thought about you, wondered where you were, why you left, who you were with, or what you were up to. The girls have tried to fix me up over the years, but it never felt right inside. Now that you are back, that part of me is thrilled, but it's also worried that too much time has passed. To be honest, Betsy," he continued, now with an edge to his voice, "The other part of me is still pissed off at you. Pissed that you never once tried to talk to me about how you felt. Pissed that you had a fling with Warren Wilson. I never told anyone, but I knew, and it hurt. It hurt even more when I read this note," he said showing her the twenty-five year old piece of stationery he had taken from his pocket. "Twenty-five years is a long time, Betsy. I just don't know if we can just pick up where we left off."

"I know what you mean, Mac. It's one of the reasons I didn't come back sooner. To be honest, if this thing with Aimee hadn't happened, God knows if I ever would have tried to re-enter your lives. If it makes a difference, there's never been anyone else for me either. I was so ashamed after the affair with Warren, that I could never bring myself to be close with anyone again. I also felt the need to constantly guard my past, which made it difficult to have many close friends."

"Well no matter what happens, Betsy, we have our three lovely daughters to keep us connected." After a short pause, he added, "We were good friends before we started dating. Let's start this new chapter in our lives by rekindling that friendship first, and then we'll see what happens. Once the media moves on to another story, and the lawyers have straightened everything out, it may be easier for us to move on and live a normal life. Does that make sense?"

"It makes perfect sense," she said smiling, putting her hand on his, as they looked into each other's eyes.

Sounds of laughter came from the kitchen, prompting Mac and Betsy to get up from their seats to see what was happening.

"It sounds like a teenage slumber party in here!" Betsy said, as they stood in the opening to the kitchen.

"Oh, good idea!" Aimee shouted. "Let's do that tonight."

"No, young lady. I think we should finally get you home to get some rest. Do I need to remind you that you were just released from the hospital this morning?"

"Aaww, Mommmm," the three girls said in unison, giggling like teenagers.

"Girls, listen to your Mother. There will be plenty of time for sleep-overs later."

Turning to Betsy, Mac asked with a large smile, "What were you saying about missing so many things?"

At that, everyone laughed themselves to tears.

Just as the family was sitting down for supper, Kevin returned from the hospital, with news about his uncle's condition. Joining everyone at the table, he explained how doctors told his uncle that his body was sending him a warning. Tests had found a blockage and an angioplasty had been scheduled for the following day. With medication, a proper diet, exercise and less stress, he had a good chance of avoiding a major heart attack. Uncle Liam would be able to relax and enjoy his retirement now that Kevin assumed total responsibility for the drug store.

"Do you think your uncle will be able to stay away from the drug store?" asked Mac.

"I don't think so, but we'll see," Kevin answered. "He may get bored sitting at home after a while. Perhaps he'll cover the bench during my vacation. Either way, I have to hire another pharmacist. Needless to say, my vacation is over. I have to return to work tomorrow."

"I think we all have to return to our normal routines," Anne said, adding, "I'm back to work on Monday."

The happy news about Uncle Liam kept the mood light around a truly "family" table for the first time in a quarter-century. Funny recollections from the past and talk about what each other had been doing filled the dining area as the sun set and the tide rose on the beach.

As predicted by Sergeant Wilson, the TV crews and reporters slowly dispersed as their on-air and print deadlines approached. Sally and Drew laughed as the last news crews quickly packed as the surf crept closer and closer, reclaiming more of the beach for the second time that day.

Around eight o'clock, the phone rang. Mac answered. Everyone in the room remained quiet, listening to Mac's side of the conversation. "Hi, Warren… yes, everyone is still here. We were just discussing bringing Betsy and Aimee to Sanford. Yes, the media has finally left as far as we can tell. That would be great… Thanks. Talk with you soon. Goodbye."

"What would be 'great' Mac?" Betsy asked.

"Warren said the patrol car outside will escort us to the town line just in case the media is waiting elsewhere. He told me Sanford Police have kept an eye on your place, and all is quiet. Are you and Aimee ready to go? I'll take you home." He looked over to Kevin and Anne, giving them a wink. "I had planned to stay here for the weekend, but let's give the newlyweds one last night of honeymoon, since Kevin's back to work tomorrow."

Everyone spent the next five minutes giving good-bye hugs. Betsy and Aimee expressed their thanks for the lovely day.

"When will we see you again, Aimee?" Drew asked.

"If things calm down, and you're mom says it's okay, how 'bout I take you both to Water Country next week?"

"Awesome!" They both answered as if rehearsed.

"Well I guess *I'm* not the 'favorite aunt' anymore," Anne said smiling.

Ever the diplomat, Sally responded, "Auntie Anne, we just have two favorite aunts, now!"

"Good answer," Aimee said, nodding in approval.

After another round of hugs at the car, Mac drove away with his long-lost wife and daughter. Back inside, Mary Beth and Anne returned to the dining room and began cleaning up and doing the dishes.

"Annie. I'm so sorry I didn't tell you and Dad about Mom. I really wanted to, but she made me promise. I was afraid she'd disappear again if I told you guys."

"I was angry with you at first, but things have worked out. I've calmed down. Mom is back, and we have a sister! I suppose I probably would have done the same thing had I been the one to find her. You're not keeping any other secrets from me, are you?"

"No, Sis, that's the only one!"

* * * * *

Once the dishes were cleaned and put away, Mary Beth took the kids home, following Mac's lead to give Kevin and Anne one last night alone.

Sitting on the deck, they finished the bottle of wine from dinner and enjoyed the moonlit night.

"It's been quite a honeymoon, Annie… one for the record books. Aren't you glad we didn't go on a cruise?"

"I think I need a vacation to recuperate from the honeymoon! In the course of two weeks, I got married, found a young woman unconscious on the beach, learned that my mother is alive and back in the area, and that the young woman is my biological sister. Not to mention you getting the drug store and your uncle going to the hospital."

Anne took a sip of the wine then started to giggle.

"What's so funny Annie?"

"Yesterday, Mary Beth said this thing with Aimee was something you'd see on a *Lifetime Movie*. I was just thinking that it really is like a plot for a *Lifetime Network Movie*."

When the bottle of wine was empty, Kevin and Anne returned inside.

Heading toward the stairs, Kevin announced, "Well, I've got an early day tomorrow… I'm going to bed!"

"Me too," answered Anne mischievously, "but I don't have an early day…"

* * * * *

In the car on the way to Sanford, Aimee carried the conversation for most of the way. She was so excited about having real family, with sisters, a dad, a brother-in-law, and a niece and nephew who thought she was cool.

Betsy directed Mac through Sanford until they reached her apartment.

"It's good to be home and finally sleep in my own bed," Aimee said as they pulled into the driveway. Then with a certain amount of sarcasm, said, "I don't know what I'll do without having someone wake me up in the middle of the night to ask me if I'm resting comfortably, though?"

"Well, take the next few days to rest. You'll need it if you're taking the kids to Water Country next week," Mac said.

"Good night, Daddy," Aimee said arching over the front seat to give him a kiss on the cheek. "See you soon?"

"Absolutely."

"Aimee, I'll meet you inside. Do you have your keys?"

"Oh, wait, no I don't. I left them in my car… oh my God, that's right, my car and things are still in a Harbor Point impound lot!"

"I'll call Warren and find out where they are." Mac volunteered. "I'll come by to give you a lift back to the beach tomorrow."

"Ooh… quality time with my dad. It's so cool having a father!"

"Here is my key," Betsy said, offering her keys to Aimee. "I'll be right in."

They watched as Aimee entered the house, seeing lights come on as she ventured through the apartment.

"She is so excited about all of this," Mac said.

"Had I known," Betsy began, with a laugh, "I would have gotten her a father a long time ago! Seriously, though, Mac, I want to thank you for everything you did today. You and the girls made this situation easy. I was so worried and scared about what it would be like. I wouldn't have blamed you if you handled things differently."

"Betsy, as I said earlier, there is a part of me that still hurts, but the other part of me is thrilled to have you back in our lives. No matter what happens, we still have our daughters."

"Yes. That's true. I'll probably see you tomorrow when you pick up Aimee."

"Hey, summer weekends usually mean 'open house' at the cottage. Mary Beth and Anne always show up when they are not working Saturday and Sunday. You and Aimee are welcome to join us, too."

"That would be great, Mac. Thanks."

The porch lights began to flash on and off, causing Betsy and Mac to look toward the house. Aimee stood in the window with a big smile on her face.

"I guess that's my cue. See you tomorrow," Betsy said as she got out of the car.

"I'll give Aimee a call. See you."

Mac waited until Betsy made it to the house. She turned, smiled and waved good-bye just before entering the house. Inside, Aimee was waiting. She had already made some tea and placed her mother's secret scrapbook on the kitchen table. "Can we look through this together now?"

* * * * *

It didn't take long for feature articles to appear in the *Maine Sunday Telegram*, and *New Hampshire Sunday News.* Once the Associated Press picked up the story, it quickly began to appear on TV stations and in newspapers across the country. Producers from the networks were calling. Everyone wanted to talk to the McDonald family –

20/20, 60 Minutes, Ellen, Leno, Conan, Letterman, Oprah, and Barbara Walters.

* * * * *

Watching the large flat screen TV in the corner of the bar, Dan "Sam" Mason watched as Suzette Jones anchoring the local "tabloid" TV news station announced – LOST AND FOUND! Missing New Hampshire woman returns after twenty-five years!

Once considered a "news babe" during her fifteen years on a Boston station, Jones now found herself on the downside of her career. Although she still anchored the news at 6 and 11, she no longer had the youthful appearance the large market stations wanted in their highly paid on-air talent.

She reported on the story Dan knew so well - the disappearance of his ex-wife's mother. He could feel the anger rise from his gut, causing a string of expletives to flow from his mouth.

"That god-damned, fuckin', bitch. That friggin' family screwed me again!"

Dan realized that by making herself known to her family, and no longer hiding in plain sight, Elizabeth Myers McDonald had squashed his blackmail attempts. He had hoped to use the tip he'd received from his girlfriend to extort some money from both Betsy and the family.

As Suzette "threw" the story to a reporter standing on Harbor Point Beach, Dan did something he had not done in months. He poured himself a shot of Jack Daniels, quickly downed it, and repeated the process multiple times. *Screw it,* he thought, now pouring the whiskey in a tall glass. By the time an old episode of "Everybody Loves Raymond," came on following the news, Dan was drunk. It had been awhile, but things had not changed. When Dan was drunk, he was a mean drunk. Some of his "regulars" tried to calm him down, but instead it made him angrier, as he started to throw punches at them. The next morning, Dan found himself hung over, in jail, and unemployed.

* * * * *

Twenty-seven hundred miles away, Joan Fitzgerald sat alone in the apartment she had hoped to once again share with her daughter Emily. Unfortunately, Emily had declared her independence by moving into her own place in Eagle.

Since then, rather than listening to Emily recount the events of her exciting day as a new lawyer at Greene & Greene, Joan had gotten into the bad habit of eating a microwaved meal while watching the evening news. Tonight was no exception. She never missed the six o'clock news and Clay Reynolds, its middle-aged anchor with rugged good looks and deep blue eyes. He was paired with Heather Hansberry, an attractive, perky, twenty-something young enough to be his daughter. There were rumors she actually was. Joan turned up the volume as Clay appeared on screen.

"We open our KBOI-2 news tonight with an amazing story from Maine, which apparently has ties to Boise."

"That's right, Clay," Heather said, picking up the story, "Twenty-five years ago, Elizabeth McDonald, disappeared from her Exeter, New Hampshire home, leaving her husband and two young daughters wondering where she was and why she left."

As Heather continued, file photos and b-roll footage courtesy of a New Hampshire television station filled the screen.

"It appears Mrs. McDonald moved to the Boise-area where she lived for seventeen years as Betsy Myers. Six months after arriving in Boise, Mrs. McDonald gave birth to a young girl she named Aimee…"

Aimee's high school yearbook photo and what appeared to be her current State of Maine driver's license photo now filled the screen, causing Joan to abruptly turn off her TV.

For twenty-five years, Joan hoped the two babies she delivered that day were fraternal twins. Tonight she learned, they could not have looked more alike. Realizing that once Emily learned the truth, she would probably never see or speak to her again, Joan began to sob.

Chapter 14

Almost everyone from G Squared was at *The Jury Room*, a high-end restaurant and bar just up the street from the firm. Emily and her colleagues were there to celebrate one of their own passing the bar exam.

"We'll be celebrating *your* achievement soon, Emily," Jason Rush said with a wink.

"I hope so, Mr. Rush," Emily replied, quickly walking away from the bar.

She had been advised by her female co-workers to stay away from the thrice-divorced partner in the firm.

"He's a slime ball. You don't want to be another one of his conquests," warned senior paralegal Cassidy Pimento. 'He believes in the 'four F's.'"

"The 'four F's?" Emily asked innocently.

"C'mon girl, you've never heard of the 'four F's'?"

"I'm pretty sure I know what one 'F' is," Emily said, "But what are the other three?"

"Girl, the 'four F's' are, 'find 'em, feel' em, fuck' em, and forget' em.'"

"Thanks for the warning Cass. I appreciate it."

"No problem. I learned the hard way. I was the *first* 'Mrs. Rush'. But remember, he's still a partner, so don't piss him off."

Over Cassidy's shoulder, she could see Rush circling several pretty summer associates, like a shark looking for its next meal.

"It's pretty late; I think I'll be heading home. See you tomorrow, Cass."

"Goodnight, Girl. Drive home safely."

It was 10:40 p.m., when she arrived at her apartment. Kicking off her shoes, she placed her briefcase and purse on the dining room table before quickly sorting through her mail.

"Perry, do you mind if we watch the eleven o'clock news before going to bed?" Emily asked her new roommate, a black and white kitten she named *Perry Mason*, after the famous TV lawyer.

Turning on the television, Emily sat on the couch and was quickly joined by her kitten, which immediately began to cuddle and purr. Clay Reynolds, her mother's favorite anchorman, was on screen with a story from Maine. When the images of Aimee Myers appeared on the screen, Emily shot to her feet, sending her surprised kitten flying across the room. She could not believe what she was seeing, and slowly sat on the edge of the sofa. Perry was already seated at her feet, waiting for an invitation to jump into her lap once again.

What the hell is going on? Why does this Aimee Myers look exactly like me?

It was 11:07, and her mother was probably asleep, but she didn't care. She had to speak to Joan right away. Activating the voice control on her iPhone, Emily said, "Call Mom." Seconds later, Joan answered the phone.

"Emily… it's late. Is everything alright?"

"I don't know Mom. You tell me. Did you watch the news tonight?

Joan lied. "I… uh… no I missed it tonight, Honey"

"C'mon Mother. I know you never miss Clay Reynolds on the six o'clock news."

"Well, I was out tonight and missed it." More lies.

Joan was trying to hold back the tears, realizing her life was about to start spinning out of control.

"Mom. I can hear you crying. You know what I'm talking about, don't you?"

"Oh, Emily. I love you so much… I love you so much. You don't realize how much I love you."

"Joan!" Emily said pointedly. "Why does that woman in Maine look like me?"

Even though Emily could not see her mother's face, she sensed something had instantly changed.

"How the fuck should I know, Emily," Joan fired back. "Is it my fault that someone *looks* like you now?"

The sudden change in her mother's demeanor and her use of the f-word, reminded Emily of the graduation day exchange that began at the Olive Garden and continued in front of her Stanford apartment. "Bad" Joan was now on the offensive.

"What's the matter? 'Miss Big Shot Lawyer' can't stand having someone fuck'n look like her now?" Joan asked sarcastically.

"Mom, what's the matter with you? Are you okay? Why are you talking like that?

"Look, kiddo. You're not supposed to throw fucking accusations around like that. Didn't they teach you that shit in law school?"

"Mom, you're really acting weird. I'm coming right over. We need to talk."

"Emily. It's really late, and frankly, I'm not in the mood to have company at this hour. By the time you get here it'll be close to midnight. Don't you need to be at "G-Whatever-you-call-it" early in the morning?"

"We call it 'G Squared', Mom, and yes, I do have an early meeting, but I'm worried about you. You don't seem to be yourself right now."

"Oh, so now all of a sudden you care about how I'm fuck'n doing? You didn't want to live with me anymore. You wanted to move into a big fancy apartment in Eagle... 'Miss High and Mighty, Big Shot Lawyer'."

"Mom, have you been drinking?"

"No, I haven't been drinking," replied Joan in a mocking tone.

"Why are you acting like this then?"

"Because I don't give a shit anymore! Except for you, my life has been one big suck-fest after another. My mom died when I was born; my father abandoned me. My foster parents never really cared when their sons sexually abused me. They were only concerned about losing the check they got from the state. Years later, my husband left me, and now you!"

"Mom, where is all this coming from?"

"You don't get it do you, Emily. It's all been a big lie. The past twenty-five years have been a BIG… FUCKING… LIE! And I'm tired of living it. Good-bye Emily."

"Mom… Mom?"

It was no use. The line was already dead. Emily hit re-dial, but all she got was a busy signal.

"I've got to get over there before she does something stupid," she said to herself.

As she drove towards her mother's apartment, Emily called the Police.

"Caldwell Police Department… Sergeant Tracy."

"Hi. My name is Emily Fitzgerald. I'm a lawyer with Greene & Greene in Eagle. I just got off the phone with my mother, and I'm concerned for her safety."

"What's the nature of your concern, Ms. Fitzgerald?"

"She's really acting weird, and I'm afraid she might try to hurt herself… or worse. I'm heading over there now. Can you have an officer meet me?"

"Yes, Ma'am. "Where does she live?

"1325 Parker Road, Apartment 2."

Do you know if she has a gun or any weapons in the house?"

"Other than the standard kitchen knives, none that I am aware of, Sergeant."

"Okay. I'll have dispatch send a car over. An officer will be waiting for you outside."

"Thank you, Sergeant."

Distraught, Joan peeked through the curtains. She knew Emily would come. She didn't expect her to bring the police though. *It's time to do this,* she thought.

Everything was laid out on the kitchen table. A letter to her daughter explaining her reasons for what she had done, and what she was about to do. She also left personal records and twenty-five year old newspaper clippings about the auto accident on the day she was born.

When Emily arrived, Joan took one last look at her through the curtains, and mouthed her last words. "I'll always love you Emily."

Police Officer Stephen Mackay was greeting Emily at her car when the shot came from the upstairs apartment. Immediately calling for back up, Mackay ran toward the second floor stairs with his gun drawn. Emily followed, keeping a safe distance behind.

When they arrived at her mother's front door, there were no signs of forced entry, but they saw a spray of blood and tissue on a nearby window and curtain.

Emily handed the officer the key to her mother's apartment. Motioning to Emily to back away, Mackay carefully opened the door then entered the apartment. Immediately, Mackay saw Joan's body slumped in the chair by the window, with a gun near her now limp hand! He immediately checked the other rooms of the two-bedroom apartment, used his radio to call for emergency personnel, although he knew it was too late.

Emily walked in and saw what was left of her mother's face. "Oh Mom… Mom. Why? Why did you do this? Why?" Then the floodgate of tears opened.

Officer Brian "Spider" Webb and his new partner, Officer Cindy Brigham, arrived on scene just as Mackay called for the ambulance. Seeing Emily in tears, Officer Brigham walked over to console and gently remove her from the apartment, allowing Webb and Mackay to secure the scene until the crime scene investigators arrived.

Brigham guided Emily toward her police cruiser, opening its back door to offer Emily a seat. As Emily slowly composed herself, Brigham asked her a few questions.

"Is there someone – a friend or relative I can call for you, Ms. Fitzgerald?"

Unfortunately, Emily no longer had a "next of kin." She hated the idea of calling her mentor at the firm. The last person she wanted to see right now was Jason Rush. Especially since he'd already had a lot to drink when she saw him two hours ago.

"No. No," Emily sniffed. "I'll be fine."

Just then, the sergeant she had spoken to on the phone arrived to take charge of the scene. Looking at Emily, he said, "Aren't you the daughter of that woman from Maine who's all over the news tonight?"

Before she could answer, Officer Mackay walked up to report the situation to Sergeant Tracy.

"Excuse us, Ms. Fitzgerald." Tracy said to Emily. "Cindy, could you stay with her? Thanks."

Walking toward the apartment with Mackay, Tracy said, "Okay, what happened?"

Mackay reported the brief scenario of hearing the gunshot, clearing the apartment, and securing the scene.

"Right now, Webb is talking to the landlady who lives in the first floor apartment," Mackay replied.

"I imagine she's a little shaken, too. I'll have Webb and Brigham talk to some of the other neighbors as well. What else we got?" Tracy asked.

"Sarge… The victim knew her daughter was coming. It looks like she left a note and a bunch of interesting stuff on the kitchen table for her to find when she arrived."

"Did you read the note? What did it say?" Tracy asked.

"Yeah. I gave it a quick glance. You know that story they've been talking about on the news tonight, Sarge?"

"Yeah, I saw the report at six."

"Wait until you read the letter!"

* * * * *

Not wanting to talk directly to her mentor at this hour, Emily called Jason Rush's office number, and left a voice mail message.

"Mr. Rush… this is Emily Fitzgerald. My mother committed suicide just before midnight. I'm at her apartment now with the police. I'm calling to

let you know that I will not be able to keep our 8:00 a.m. meeting, and I'll
need a few days to make arrangements. Good-bye."

Thankful for voicemail, she was surprised when her phone rang a
minute later, his name appearing on the screen.

Cautiously answering, she said, "Hello, this is Emily Fitzgerald."

"Emily… it's Jason. I'm sooo sorry to hear about your mother. Are
you okay? Is there anything I can do?"

He was slurring his words quite a bit, and she wondered if he
would even remember speaking to her in the morning.

"Thank you, Mr. Rush. I…"

He interrupted. "Emily, please call me Jason."

"Thank you, Jason. I'll be fine, but I'll call you should I need
anything. I really just wanted to let you know what happened and that I
need to take a few days off."

"Please… take as much time as you need."

"Thank you for understanding, Jason."

"Are you sure there's *nothing* I can do for you *tonight*?" he asked,
adding. "I've got a great big shoulder to cry on."

Emily wanted to gag. "No sir. I'm fine. Thank you. I've got to go."

* * * * *

Inside Joan's apartment, the CSI team checked for evidence that
might point to anything other than a self-inflicted gunshot wound to the
head. Although the medical examiner's initial on-site findings were

consistent with that of a suicide, he still needed to bring Joan's body to the morgue for further examination and testing to confirm those findings.

Emily stood on the sidewalk outside her mother's apartment, while the team of investigators worked inside. Two hours later, Emily watched the medical examiner and his assistant remove the body bag containing her mother's body from the apartment.

Although she had many friends and co-workers, Emily realized she no longer had a family. *It's official. I am alone in this world,* she thought, as tears began to stream down her lightly freckled cheeks once again.

Sergeant Tracy found her in the driveway, leaning against her mother's car.

"Ms. Fitzgerald," he said, calling her over with his fingers. "Your mother was apparently expecting you to come. She left a note and other information I think you'll want to see."

"Yes, Sergeant. I told her I was coming, although she said she didn't want company at this hour."

"What made you decide to come *at this late hour?*" he asked.

"I saw the news story about the woman in Maine and her daughter's picture. The daughter looks like me. I think you noticed that too, when you arrived here earlier. Didn't you?"

"Yes, I was about to mention it when Officer Mackay walked up."

"Anyway, when I saw her photo, I called my mother to ask her if she knew anything about this, especially with the woman's Boise-area connection. Mom always acted funny when I asked about my father, her lack of family members, etc. She was always overly protective of me, and my background. Lately, when we spoke, her personality would suddenly change. She became mean. Every sentence included the f-word, and she seemed to resent that I became a lawyer and wanted to live in my own apartment."

"Well, Ms. Fitzgerald," Tracy began, "I'm sure the autopsy will identify if something was causing those personality swings. Dr. Drake is quite thorough with his investigations."

Taking a breath, the sergeant said, "I imagine you'd like to see what she wanted you to find."

"Yes, sir. I would."

"As an attorney, I'm sure you realize everything is considered evidence, so I can't leave you alone with the stuff she left for you."

"I do. Thank you, Sergeant."

"I need to get back to the station, but I'll have Officer Brigham stay here with you."

Wearing the latex gloves Sergeant Tracy gave to her, Emily picked up her mother's suicide note, now encased in a plastic protective sleeve. There was no doubt her mother had written the letter. It was definitely her handwriting. She began to read.

Dear Emily,

As I write this letter, I know you're on your way here, and since you're reading this, you already know I'm dead. I loved you so much. You were my life - my purpose - for the past twenty-five years. I'm very proud of the beautiful, successful young woman you've become. I ended my life tonight because of that story on the news. Once you learn the truth, and I've left it all on the table for you, my life would have been over anyway.

The truth is, Emily, that young woman in Maine – the one that looks so much like you – is your twin sister. Her mother - is your <u>real mother</u>. I delivered both of you in my ambulance after she was in a car accident. She thought she was only having one baby. She never knew about you. So I secretly kept you and raised you as my own, hoping that this day would never come. I had always wanted a baby but could never have one on my own. It's why my husband left me. I thought it had been God's way of giving me a child to love and to be loved.

Please forgive me for depriving you of a life with your real family. I was selfish - always wanting to keep your love and attention for myself because I never received it from anyone else.

Remember, Emily - this woman (and her family) doesn't know about you. They are going through their own healing process right now. Keep this in mind before you try to contact them – as I know you will. It may re-open a wound that will only cause you more harm.

Love,

~~Mom~~ Joan

Using her sleeves to wipe the tears from her face, Emily began looking at everything Joan had left behind. There were old newspaper clippings about the accident on the day she was born. According to the article, it had been a pretty severe accident. The woman – her birth mother, had to be removed using the "jaws of life." The other driver had died at the scene. The photos of the accident were gruesome.

Joan had been featured in one of the articles for having successfully delivered the woman's baby. Apparently Joan had delivered many babies as an EMT, earning her the nickname, "Stork" Fitzgerald. *I never knew that*, she thought, smiling.

It was all there. Every memento of Emily's life with the woman she called 'Mom' was on this table. It was like a time capsule of her life. Inside she found a collection of handmade greeting cards, grade school artwork, report cards, certificates and awards she had earned, and long forgotten, and more news clippings.

Joan had kept a journal recording everything she had done from the day she placed Emily inside the cooler to her final entry moments before she took her own life.

Reading the early entries, Emily began taking notes, writing down important dates, names, places, and activities. Two days after delivering Emily, Joan stole a copy of Aimee Myers's birth certificate and a blank form to create one for Emily Fitzgerald. Joan had told the truth in her suicide note. Emily was not a Fitzgerald, but a Myers… no; wait… according to the news report, her real last name was McDonald. Her birth mother's first name was Elizabeth. *That explains why my middle name is Elizabeth*, she thought.

The sun was starting to peak over the eastern horizon. Emily had been sitting at the kitchen table for nearly four hours, taking it all in, learning about a past she knew nothing about.

Officer Cindy Brigham had not said a word to her the entire time, but as her shift neared its end, the officer cleared her throat and said, "Ms. Fitzgerald, we need to finish up here. Once the investigation is closed, you'll have access to this material and the apartment."

"Of course, I understand," replied Emily. "Is Sergeant Tracy still on duty? I'd like to speak with him."

Using her radio, Officer Brigham contacted the station to inquire about the sergeant's duty status. "He's still at the station. Would you like me to ask him to call your cellphone?"

"Yes. That would be great. Thanks."

Five minutes later, Emily's phone rang.

"Ms. Fitzgerald, it's Sergeant Tracy. What can I do for you?"

"Thank you for calling Sergeant. I've spent the night reviewing everything my mother left on the kitchen table. I know you've read the suicide note. I'm sure you can imagine what'll happen if that information gets out to the media. I don't want Ms. Myers or her daughter Aimee to learn about my existence from some reporter."

"The Department prides itself on its ability to maintain confidentiality, Ms. Fitzgerald."

"I hope so, Sergeant. I'd rather not need to request a gag order on this case."

"No problem. Detective Mitchell Downey has been assigned the case. He should be contacting you today."

"Thank you. I'll be waiting for his call."

Before leaving, Emily walked to her old room. She hadn't seen it since her mother had redecorated it, expecting her to move back in after college. *Joan was right. It did look nice*, she thought.

Officer Brigham locked and sealed the door to the apartment. It was still considered a crime scene for now. After a long night, the two women left, each returning to their homes. Officer Brigham's shift may have ended, but things for Emily were just getting started.

When Mary Beth and Anne had moved out on their own, Mac started having weekly one-on-one chats with each of his daughters to keep in touch. While they often saw each other at the beach house on weekends, these chats were his way of staying connected to them individually. As a former military man, Mac was so accustomed to using acronyms that he eventually started referring to these "quality time with Dad" chats as "QTD's." The name stuck, and each week he would have QTD's with Mary Beth and Anne, having lunch or coffee at a nearby Panera Bread or Starbucks. Today's QTD, however, was at Mary Beth's house.

After the usual opening banter, Mary Beth asked, "I imagine you've heard about Dan?"

"Yeah… sounds like he fell off the goddamn wagon again," Mac replied, showing his dislike of his former son-in-law.

"It seems that way," Mary Beth replied. "Apparently something on TV set him off. He started doing shots and didn't stop. When his friends noticed what he was doing, the pub's regulars tried to stop him, but he started throwing punches at them. They called the cops, and he ended up in jail. I heard he got fired, too! Looks like I won't be receiving child support payments for a while."

Nodding, Mac said, "A buddy of mine was in the bar when it happened. Knowing Dan's connection to me, he called me. Fred said it started when the story of your mother's return was all over the news. He told me Dan started swearing up a storm, saying all kinds of shit about us. When I heard he was taken to jail, I called Wilson to see if he had any information. Wilson made a few phone calls and found out Dan was pissed that your mother had made herself known to us. Apparently, someone had been calling your mother threatening to reveal her secret if she did not give him money. Putting two and two together, Wilson thought Dan might be the guy. He was right. Dan admitted it."

"Great. That means Dan's going to be in jail for a while. I'll never get a cent of child support from him again." Trying to hold back tears, Mary Beth added, "Looks like I'll need to get a second job."

Mac put his hand on hers, saying, "Mary Beth, I paid a good portion of Annie's college, and I never really offered to help you, because I knew Dan would probably piss the money away on his booze and bullshit." Reaching into his shirt pocket, he said, "I'd like to make up for all those years I took you for granted. Here's a check equal to the amount I gave your sister for college."

Opening the folded check, Mary Beth could no longer hold back the tears. "Dad, this is so generous. I...I... I can probably pay off my mortgage with this!"

"That's what I figured, Pumpkin," he replied using his childhood pet name for her. "With your house paid off, you should have no problem taking care of your family, with or without child support from that loser."

Mary Beth gave him a hug, saying, "Thank you, Dad. I love you."

Returning the hug, Mac replied, "I love you too, Pumpkin."

Chapter 15

Joan Fitzgerald's remains were released by the medical examiner two weeks after her suicide. They were still waiting for several autopsy test results but everything clearly pointed to suicide. The coroner had found early signs of Atherosclerosis - hardening of the arteries, but for the most part, Joan was in good health. Joan's letter made everything pretty clear. In her mind, her life was over, so she ended it.

Joan had pre-arranged her funeral, requesting a simple gravesite service with a few words of committal before burial by a non-denominational minister. Although Joan believed in the existence of God, she never practiced a particular faith. As a child, Emily remembered sitting next to her mother as they watched Joel Osteen, or Robert Schuller's "Hour of Power" on television. Occasionally they would tune in to EWTN, the Catholic Network, and listen as priests would discuss and answer questions about their faith. She remembered watching Pope John Paul II celebrate Mass in Denver with thousands of young people from around the world. Even at her young age, Emily sensed that John Paul II was special. Something he said in his homily that day had touched her heart. She did not remember what it was, but somehow she felt spiritually energized whenever she thought about that day.

Two dozen or so people attended Joan's service at the Canyon Hill Cemetery, including her boss, co-workers, a few of her friends and neighbors. Emily was surprised when an elderly man introduced himself as Ron Fitzgerald, Joan's ex-husband. She had never met the man, but he seemed overly emotional for someone who divorced Joan thirty years ago. *He's probably hoping Joan remembered him in her will,* she thought. Most of the attendees, however, were there for Emily. A number of her co-workers from G Squared, including Jason Rush, had come to pay their last respects. Of course, hoping she might be vulnerable, the sleazy mentor took the opportunity to "hit-on" her, suggesting she join him at his Sun Valley condo for the weekend. It was an offer that Emily politely and professionally, shot down.

After a short prayer and moment of silence, Joan's casket was lowered into the grave. Dabbing tears from her eyes, Emily thanked everyone for coming. In silence, the attendees slowly returned to their cars leaving Emily alone with her thoughts.

* * * * *

In Maine, the remainder of the summer was as advertised. Weekends meant 'open house' at the McDonald cottage on Harbor Point Beach. Mary Beth, Anne, Kevin, and the kids joined Mac whenever they could. Betsy and Aimee soon became weekend regulars as well. As time passed, they no longer felt like guests at the beach house, but "at home."

Of course, like most families, happiness is sometimes marred by an errant comment - opening old wounds, causing anger, disappointment, and hurt feelings. The McDonald family was by no means immune. The stress of the media attention and everything surrounding the family's situation created occasional tension within the family, albeit short-lived.

Labor Day meant the end of school vacation for Sally and Drew. Aimee returned to her classroom to start a new year with a new group of students. She hardly knew them, but thanks to all of the TV coverage, her class certainly knew her.

The lazy summer weekends had quickly turned into busy fall weekends, and it was time to close up the beach house for the season. The McDonald family now spent weekends sitting in the bleachers to watch Sally and Drew compete in their respective sports. Occasionally, Anne and Kevin would host a tailgate-style barbecue at their new home in Kittery, where everyone stopped by to watch either Northeastern or the Patriots play football.

Things had progressed like a romance novel for Mac and Betsy. Long walks, quiet dinners, and shared reminisces of their past together, rekindled their love for each other. Weekends became long weekends, and finally, Betsy confided to Aimee that she would soon have their apartment to herself, explaining that she and her father would be living together again under one roof, and that roof was in Portsmouth.

Attorney Greenville had finally guided the paperwork through the court system. Elizabeth Myers McDonald was once again officially recognized as a living soul the eyes of the State of New Hampshire and the government of the United States of America. Since Mac had never divorced her, they were still legally married.

"Mom... you and Daddy should renew your vows. Wouldn't that be romantic?"

"Yes, Aimee it would. We were actually thinking of doing something like that on Thanksgiving Day. It seems appropriate."

"Let me take care of everything!"

"Aimee… first of all, we want it simple. There is not much to do. I've already spoken with Father Peter, and he has agreed to bless our marriage at the house before Thanksgiving dinner."

"Why don't you work with your sisters to plan, coordinate and cook the meal?"

"Do they know about you and Daddy yet?"

"Not yet. We plan on telling everyone the next time we're all together, which may be on Sunday. Kevin invited us to their house to watch the Patriots play "his" Chicago Bears. As usual, it's an open house, so if you don't have plans, I'm sure you're invited too."

* * * * *

That Sunday, the New England Patriots were trouncing the Chicago Bears 33 – 0 at half time. Everyone in the room was in a happy mood except the two Chicagoans - Kevin and his Uncle Liam.

"Belichick is probably cheating again," taunted Kevin.

"Yeah. I can remember when we beat the crap out of your Patriots in the '86 Super Bowl!" Uncle Liam said, adding to the fire.

"What have they done for you lately, Uncle Liam?" teased Annie, as she entered the room to announce lunch was available in the dining room.

As everyone gathered around a buffet table full of 'tailgate' foods Annie had prepared, Mac cleared his throat and said, "Betsy and I have an announcement!"

Taking her hand into his, he continued, "Your mother and I have decided it's time to live together again. She'll be moving her things into *our* house this week."

"We also thought it would be a nice idea to renew our vows on Thanksgiving Day," Betsy said, adding, "Father Peter has agreed to stop by and do a little ceremony for us."

Conversation immediately erupted as the three daughters began to offer their congratulations and ideas for the ceremony.

"Girls…" Mac said, making the 'quiet down' motion with his two hands. "We want the ceremony to be simple, so Mom and I will take care of that. We'd like you girls to handle the planning and preparation of Thanksgiving dinner."

"We can certainly do that," Mary Beth said, answering for her sisters.

Mac, Kevin, Uncle Liam, and Mary Beth's son, Drew, went back to the living room just as Bears kicked off to start the second half of the game. With the game so lopsided in favor of the Pats, Betsy joined her three daughters and granddaughter Sally in the kitchen to talk about Thanksgiving Dinner "must haves" and possible recipes for something new. It would be their first Thanksgiving as a family in over twenty-five years, and they all wanted to make it special.

"Mom," asked Annie, "Do you mind if Uncle Liam joins us? His wife Sandra passed away in January, so he's all alone this year."

"I don't see why not. He's part of your family," Betsy replied, "Why don't you invite Kevin's parents to join us too."

"Oh, I'm sure they'd love to. They haven't seen us since the wedding," Anne said.

"Mom, do you think Father Peter will want to stay for dinner?" asked Aimee.

"I'll offer but he often goes to the St. Agnes Senior Home to have Thanksgiving dinner with the residents. We'll have to see what he says."

Annie pulled out her cookbooks for her Mom and Mary Beth, while Aimee and Sally checked out *Pinterest* and AllRecipes.com on Aimee's iPad.

* * * * *

Following Joan's funeral, Emily became laser-focused on studying for the Idaho Bar Exam in late July. Nothing else mattered. She wanted to pass it on her first try, and the preparations kept her mind off of other things. She figured she had plenty of time to review everything Joan had left her *after* the exam.

More than once, her mentor Jason Rush tried his best to seduce his promising, young, attractive attorney, and each time, Emily politely fended off his advances. Shortly after the fourth of July, however, he took his advances to a higher level. Late one evening, Emily was in the firm's law library, when he suddenly came up from behind her and placed his hands on her breasts as he nuzzled the back of her neck. Instinctively she used several self-defense techniques she had learned while at Stanford. Before he realized what was happening, Emily had Rush on the floor with his right arm held tightly behind his back.

"Emily, I have to admit this is really hot, but you're hurting me."

"Mr. Rush. I've given you enough warnings. If you touch me again, you'll be in even more pain."

"Emily… Emily," Rush said condescendingly. "Who's going to believe you? I'm a partner."

"I will," Linus Greene, the firm's founder said as he swiveled the high backed executive chair revealing his presence to the junior partner.

"Oh … Hello, Mr. Greene. I didn't see you sitting there. I was just kidding around with Ms. Fitzgerald. You know… just trying to keep her loose for her upcoming bar exam."

"Ms. Fitzgerald, would you please excuse me and Mr. Rush?"

"Yes sir. I will. Just let me collect my things," Emily said, quickly sliding her study materials into her briefcase.

"Goodnight, Mr. Greene. Goodnight, Mr. Rush."

"One more thing, Ms. Fitzgerald. Please stop my office when you get in tomorrow morning."

"Yes, sir."

Emily quickly left the library. After the heavy wooden door closed behind her, she leaned against it, slowly exhaling a deep cleansing breath. As she walked away, she could tell her sleazy mentor was getting his ass handed to him. It sounded as though he was being fired. *Good, the sonofabitch deserves it,* she thought while walking towards the parking lot.

The next morning Emily met with Mr. Greene as requested. Joining them was Rebecca Gould, the firm's Senior Vice President of Human Resources. After answering their questions, Emily learned that Jason Rush had been placed on administrative leave pending the results of an investigation into his 'bad habits' with women. Apparently, two of the three summer associates Emily had seen Rush circle like a hungry shark at The Jury Room had reported him as well.

"Don't worry, Emily," the firm's founder said. "He's cleaning out his desk this morning. I've had enough of his shenanigans, and thanks to you, we now have enough to prove it."

"Thank you, Mr. Greene. I'll be at my desk if you need me."

"By the way Ms. Fitzgerald," the HR chief said, "If Jason Rush bothers you outside of this building, don't be afraid to call the police. I'd rather you let the police handle Rush, although from what I've heard, you can take care of yourself."

Emily could not help but notice a slight smile on her face as she made that last comment.

"Thank you, Ms. Gould. I will," she said, adding as she left the room, "Hopefully, I won't need to."

* * * * *

Emily sat for the two-day Idaho State Bar Examination in late July. With the drama of her mother's suicide and her former mentor's constant sexual advances behind her, she was prepared and focused. Confident she had done well, Emily moved on with her life, not worrying about test results she would receive in November.

During the day, Emily assisted on several important cases, sitting in the courtroom alongside Greene & Greene's best attorneys, while gaining valuable experience. She impressed everyone she worked with, and she became somewhat of a hero to the other young women Jason Rush had harassed at G Squared. At night and on weekends, she slowly went through her mother's papers, uncovering secrets about her past, and learning things about the woman she had called "Mom" for nearly twenty-six years. Joan's early life had certainly been rough, but in many ways, Emily was proud of what Joan had accomplished as an adult. She had risen through the ranks through hard work and determination to become Director of Emergency Medical Services for the Caldwell Fire and Rescue Department.

By the time Labor Day arrived, Emily had culled through everything Joan had left. That weekend, Emily sold most of Joan's things at a yard sale, donating the proceeds to the Caldwell Fire and Rescue Department's EMT Scholarship Fund in Joan's name. Emily kept a few things, though, like the box of Christmas ornaments she and Joan had collected over the years, and the furniture Joan had recently purchased to redecorate her childhood bedroom.

* * * * *

After reading Joan's personal papers, Emily had hired a private investigator to find out everything about Betsy and Aimee Myers' life in Boise, as well as their current situation in New England. The Red Rope expandable folder containing his report and materials had been sitting unopened on the corner of her desk for nearly two months. A part of her wanted to learn everything about her real family, while another part seemed reluctant to do so.

Lying awake, unable to sleep one night, several of Emily's old memories now began to make sense. As a teenager, people would often say "Hey, Aimee," when they passed her at the mall, or at another public place, looking puzzled as to why she did not acknowledge them in kind. Back then she never understood why people kept calling her Aimee. Now she knew, thinking *No shit Sherlock, you have an identical twin*. She remembered one possible close encounter with Aimee at a high school football game against Boise High. She was wearing her Caldwell High sweatshirt when some guy walked up to her near the concession stand saying, "Hey, Aimee, why the fuck are you wearing that Caldwell sweatshirt? Didn't I just see you over there wearing Jay's varsity jacket?" She had wanted to see this Aimee girl, but venturing into the "home" bleachers wearing Caldwell High gear was not a smart idea. But now, there were no "home bleachers" preventing her from meeting Aimee or her mother. Still unable to sleep, Emily padded into her living room, sat at her desk, turned on the desk lamp, and dove into the investigator's in-depth two reports.

The first dossier she opened focused on Elizabeth (Betsy) Maureen O'Connor McDonald (Myers).

Emily stared at the driver's license photo on the first page. It was the face of her birth mother. The woman who had carried her for nine months but did not know she existed. She had short, light gray hair, deep blue eyes, and a nice complexion for a woman of her age. Elizabeth was still an attractive woman. Emily realized she had her mother's eyes, nose and chin. According to the driver's license, Elizabeth was five feet, three inches tall, and weighed 135 pounds. She was also an organ donor. *Good for you, Elizabeth!* Emily thought, as she continued to read.

Born: November 12, 1946 (Age 67), Manchester, New Hampshire

Married: Richard "Mac" McDonald (May 30, 1965)

Children: Mary Elizabeth McDonald Mason (DOB: February 23, 1973)

      Anne Mary McDonald Burke (DOB: September 14, 1985)

      Aimee Michelle Myers (DOB: June 2, 1988)

      Emily Elizabeth Fitzgerald* (DOB: June 2, 1988)

Attended: St. Joseph's Catholic School, Manchester, NH (Grades 1-12)

      College of Southern Idaho-Boise – Associate Degree, Accounting

Occupation: Bookkeeper, St. Christopher's Church, Sanford, ME

Residences: 322-B Mill Street, Sanford, ME (2007 – Present)

      1045 East Street, Concord, NH (2003 – 2007)

1248 North 30th Street, Apt 10, Boise, ID (1988 – 2003)

215 Epping Road, Exeter, NH (1967 – 1988)

91 South Beech Street, Manchester, NH (1965 – 1967)

100 Chestnut Street, Manchester, NH (1946 - 1965)

Father: Joseph Michael O'Connor (1920 – 1986)

Married: Elizabeth Mary Myers (September 1945)

Occupation: Mailman

Mother: Elizabeth (Betty) Myers O'Connor (1922 – 1985)

Married: Joseph M. O'Connor (September 1945)

Occupation: Homemaker

The remainder of the dossier contained a narrative about Elizabeth O'Connor McDonald (Myers) disappearance from New Hampshire in 1988, the subsequent investigation and search for her by local authorities, and the fact that she had been declared dead in 1995. It also included a similar narrative about the life of Elizabeth Myers in Boise, Idaho, and the severe car accident and birth of a child following that accident. These accounts were created based on old and recent newspaper articles and interviews conducted by the private investigator. Copies of the articles and transcripts of the interviews were included in the folder. At Emily's request, the investigator did not contact or interview anyone closely related to the McDonald family.

It was now 6:00 a.m., and a cold, heavy rain began to fall, just as the meteorologists had predicted, calling it a perfect day to sleep in, or curl up in a chair with a good book. That's exactly what Emily was doing, except this was no James Patterson novel. This was a "ripped from the headlines" story, with a *Lifetime Movie Network twist,* Emily thought. If she only knew her older sisters, who lived twenty-seven hundred miles away, often made the same comparison to their situation.

With a fresh cup of coffee in hand, Emily opened the second dossier containing information about Aimee Michelle Myers. Once again, a driver's license photo stared back at her. This one, however, was like looking into a mirror. Her shoulder length hair was auburn in color, and she, too, had deep blue eyes and a straight nose. *My God,* thought Emily *she even has my cute freckles*! According to the license, Aimee was five foot, five inches tall and weighed 125 pounds. The only difference she noticed was their weight. Emily weighed in at 115.

Born: June 2, 1988 (Age 25), Boise, ID

Marital Status: Single

Children: None

Attended: Boise, ID Public Schools (Pre-K to 12)

                 Plymouth State University, Plymouth, NH – BA, Early Education (2010)

Occupation: Elementary School Teacher, Sanford, ME Public School System

Residences: 322-B Mill Street, Sanford, ME (2007 – Present)

1045 East Street, Concord, NH (2003 – 2007)

1248 North 30th Street, Apt 10, Boise, ID (1988 – 2003)

Father: Richard "Mac" McDonald (April 15, 1943 -)

Married: Elizabeth O'Connor (May 30, 1965)

Occupation: Lt. Colonel, NH Air National Guard (Retired)

Mother: Elizabeth (Betsy) Maureen O'Connor (Myers) (November 12, 1946 -)

Married: Richard "Mac" McDonald (May 30, 1965)

Occupation: Bookkeeper

Siblings: Mary Elizabeth McDonald Mason (DOB: February 23, 1973)

Anne Mary McDonald Burke (DOB: September 14, 1985)

Emily Elizabeth Fitzgerald* (DOB: June 2, 1988)

Similar to Elizabeth's dossier, there were newspaper clippings, photos, and other things mentioning Aimee Myers, including the page from her high school yearbook.

Aimee Michelle Myers –

"Don't cry because it's over, smile because it happened."
– Dr. Seuss

Honor Roll 1, 2, 3, 4 Future Teachers of America 1, 2, 3, 4, Cross-Country 2, 3, 4 Drama Club 2, 3, 4, National Honor Society 3, 4, Student Council 3, 4

Perry, Emily's kitten jumped onto her lap, begging for attention. Stroking his fur, Emily said, "My sister certainly participated in a lot of extra-curricular activities, Perry! I never got to do that much in high school." Joan had limited Emily's school activities to things like student government and the library club, saying these activities would help her get into law school more than sports would. Emily now understood why Joan had been so over-protective. Knowing Emily had a twin sister in the area, she had been constantly afraid the two girls might somehow cross paths as the unknowing twins did at summer camp in *Disney's The Parent Trap.*

After reviewing all of the materials in the folder, Emily desperately wanted to meet Aimee, her sisters and her *real* parents… her family. Beyond that, she had no expectations. Emily just wanted to let them know she existed. Her life was in Idaho, not New England, and she had no plans to move east. Before simply showing up on the McDonald's doorstep, Emily thought it might be a good idea to speak with someone first, and she knew exactly who that would be. It was a name that appeared in *everything* she had been reading.

Chapter 16

She had met the man once or twice before, and Joan had introduced him as her brother.

"I guess that makes me your uncle, young lady," the tall man in uniform said, smiling as he crouched to shake her little hand.

In her mind, Emily could hear herself as a little girl asking Joan about him.

"Mommy… I didn't know you had a brother."

"Yes, I do Sweetheart," Joan had explained, "He's my only brother, and he's two years older than me. When my Grandma Alice died, we were sent to different foster families. I was too young to write letters to him then, so we lost touch until a few years ago."

Although they both seemed happy to have reconnected after that one visit, their reunion eventually became nothing more than an exchange of Christmas cards every year. *Joan could never get a relationship to stick*, Emily thought.

* * * * *

Emily kept entering his phone number only to end the call before it connected. "How do you even begin a conversation like this?" she asked herself. Finally, summoning up the strength, she placed the call, this time letting it ring until someone answered.

"Detective Wilson," the voice answered in a confident tone.

"Hi… Uncle Warren? It's your niece… Emily Fitzgerald… Joan's daughter."

"Oh… Hi, Emily. Is everything alright?" Wilson asked cautiously. "It's been what… fifteen years?"

"Actually, I think it's more like twenty," Emily replied, beginning to feel more at ease. "I was almost six when you came to visit my… mother."

"What can I do for you Emily? Is your mother okay?"

Taking a breath, Emily launched into what sounded like an opening statement in a courtroom. After explaining that his sister had committed suicide, Emily expertly laid out the facts, starting with everything Joan admitted to in her suicide note, then she moved to the facts she had corroborated using the information found by the private investigator.

She ended by saying, "The only thing I don't have, Sergeant Wilson, are DNA test results to conclusively prove that Elizabeth and Richard McDonald are indeed my parents."

Wilson had remained quiet throughout Emily's monologue. He was very impressed with her apparent preparation and delivery. Each time he would jot down a question, she would eventually answer it without being asked a few seconds later. As she spoke, Wilson used his department laptop to search for her records with Idaho Department of Motor Vehicles. Within seconds, Emily Elizabeth Fitzgerald's driver's license appeared on the screen. *Ho-lee shit!* There was no denying whose twin sister she was, and just like Aimee, she looked a little like Anne as well. *How many more surprises can this family take?*

When Emily stopped talking, Wilson paused, then, said, "It seems I'm not really your uncle, and I'm guessing… you became a lawyer. Your presentation of the facts was excellent, young lady."

"Thank you… Sergeant."

"Please, call me Warren," he said before asking his next question. "So, Counselor, what is your next step? What do you plan to do with this information?"

A little smile appeared on her face, when he called her 'counselor.' "That's the other reason I wanted to speak with you, Warren. You've been involved with this family since this all started. I was hoping you might be able to give me some advice on how best to approach them."

He wondered if she knew how far back he had been involved with the family – especially his short-lived affair with Betsy.

"Emily, I can tell you they've accepted everything and are moving forward as one happy family. I'm not quite sure how much more they can take, but, I'll say this much – they are good people, who have been through a lot in the past twenty-five years." He went on to share with her everything that was not in the media. Finally, he asked, "So, Emily… what are your intentions and expectations?"

"I simply want to meet my *real* family and let them know that I exist," she answered. "Other than that, I have no expectations. My life is here in Idaho… but it would be nice to have family back east!"

* * * * *

Along the streets and byways of New England, autumn's colorful foliage had already fallen, leaving only the dark silhouettes of mighty oaks and maples against November's cold, steel gray skies. Thanksgiving Day had finally arrived, although one might think it was already Christmas by the look of the stores and some homes in the neighborhood whose owners already "decked their halls."

On Woodbury Avenue in Portsmouth, the McDonald home was bright and filled with activity. The aromas of roasted turkey, apple pie, and fresh, homemade bread made its way to the family room, where Sally and Drew watched the Macy's Thanksgiving Day Parade.

Mac and Betsy welcomed Kevin's parents, who had flown in from Chicago for the long holiday weekend. A fully recovered Uncle Liam joined them as well, sharing photographs from his recent Caribbean cruise.

Father Peter O'Donnell, pastor of St. Christopher Parish in Sanford, where Betsy worked, arrived shortly before noon as requested. Upon entering the home, he noted the warmth of the family and commented on the wonderful aromas emanating from the kitchen.

"You're welcome to join us for dinner, Father," Mac responded.

"Thank you, Mac, he said, "I would love to, but Betsy knows, I promised the good women at St. Agnes Senior Home that I would share their holiday meal with them. I hope you understand."

"Of course we do, Father."

"Should we get started then?"

As the large grandfather clock in the foyer chimed the noon hour, Mac and Betsy joined Father Peter in front of the fireplace. With members of their extended family looking on, Father Peter began the simple service.

Crossing himself, he began, "In the name of the Father, the Son, and the Holy Spirit…The Lord said, 'When two or more of you are gathered in My Name, I am there with you.' And so, here we stand in the presence of God and members of the McDonald and Burke families to bless the marriage and renew the sacred vows, which Richard and Betsy recited to each other many years ago."

The three girls dabbed their eyes at the sight of their parents reuniting after twenty-five years. Anne stood alongside Kevin, holding his arm, thinking about the incredible six months that had just passed. Her own wedding, the start of their honeymoon, finding Aimee on the beach, learning about her mother's twenty-five years in hiding, and now this… *what a year this has been*, she thought.

Mac surprised everyone by presenting Betsy with a new anniversary ring of diamonds.

Father Peter ended the service with a short prayer and a final blessing for the entire family. Everyone in the room offered congratulatory applause, handshakes and kisses. Kevin offered a toast as everyone lifted champagne glasses to the ceiling.

An hour later, the family sat around the extended dining room table. Everyone at the table knew the reasons they all had to be thankful this Thanksgiving, so they chose to keep things simple by offering the reciting *Grace*, before the meal. As the last syllable of 'Amen' filtered through the room, serving dishes filled with seasonal favorites were passed around the table in a well-choreographed fashion. Not a single serving bowl seemed to touch the table until everyone had an opportunity to choose what they wanted.

Laughter and good conversation filled the dining room. In her mind, Aimee thought back to her days as a young child, when she watched

TV families celebrating Thanksgiving in special holiday episodes, always hoping, but never imagining that she would someday celebrate with a large family of her own.

As they cleared the table of dishes in preparation for dessert and coffee, the doorbell rang.

"It must be Warren," Mac announced getting up from his chair, "He told me he had something to show us, so I invited him to join us for dessert," he added over his shoulder as he headed toward the front door.

Mac opened the front door to greet his old friend. "Warren… Happy Thanksgiving! C'mon in out of the cold, you're just in time for…"

Warren just stood there, knowing Mac was looking at the attractive young woman walking up behind him. A look of shock and disbelief replaced Mac's big smile as Emily raised her face to look him in the eye. She was fashionably dressed in a casual style. Long, auburn colored hair gently framed her face as it cascaded down to her shoulders. Her light complexion, deep blue eyes, and slightly freckled nose, was certainly something Mac had seen before. Cradling a large manila envelope in her left arm, she offered her outstretched right hand to Mac.

"Mr. McDonald, my name is Emily Fitzgerald, and I have reason to believe that I am your daughter – Aimee's twin sister."

"P-Pl-Please come in," Mac stammered, as Betsy walked into the foyer to also greet their guest.

"What's taking you guys so long, Mac?" Betsy asked. "What is it?"

"Congratulations… It's a girl!" he replied, motioning for Emily and Warren to enter the house.

"What do you mean it's a g…?" she asked as Emily walked through the door. Seeing her, Betsy let out a gasp loud enough to silence the happy, cheer-filled conversation in the nearby dining room, causing everyone to rush to see what had happened. Within seconds, the entire family crowded into the entrance hall seeing Mac and Warren steadying a still shocked and bewildered Betsy. Next to them stood a woman they did not know, but who obviously had a familiar face.

With everyone speechless, Wilson decided to make the introduction quick and simple, "Girls, meet your sister, Emily."

From out of the cluster, Aimee rushed to Emily like a moth to a flame, saying, "I knew it. I knew it… I knew it… I knew it."

For the first time in more than twenty-five years, the two twin sisters were together. Emily let the manila envelope drop to the floor as she opened her arms to greet her twin sister.

"I've always had *a feeling* you were out there," Aimee said, hugging her twin again. "Caldwell High School right?" she asked.

"Yeah, how did you know?" Emily asked.

"I dunno… I *just knew*. And everyone kept telling me I had a doppelganger at Caldwell High."

Aimee accepted this moment with open arms, but for some, it only opened recently healed wounds. Anne looked at Mary Beth with a furrowed brow, a look that asked *did you know about this little secret too?* Understanding the un-spoken communication with her sister, Mary Beth innocently shook her head and mouthed the word, "No!"

Watching his two youngest daughters reunite, Mac sternly whispered to Betsy, "How could you not know about *her*? What other secrets are you still hiding?"

"None! I knew nothing about her, Mac, I swear. I had no idea I was carrying twins. My doctor only heard one heartbeat, and we only saw one baby on the ultrasound."

Noticing the uneasiness, Wilson tried to lighten the mood saying, "Hey… you guys invited me over for dessert. Where's this delicious pumpkin pie I've been hearing so much about?"

A smattering of laughter followed, and everyone began to slowly walk back to the dining room. Still in the foyer, Betsy walked up to Emily, giving her a cautious and rather awkward hug, as tears began to roll down her face.

"I'm so sorry I didn't know about you…" Betsy's voice cracked, as she hugged her 'new' daughter tighter.

"It's okay, M…" Emily hesitated, not knowing exactly how to refer to her birth mother at the moment.

Aimee, who still standing at Emily's side, picked up on the hesitation and said, "It's okay, Emily, call her Mom."

"Yes, please do," said Betsy who took a step back to take in both of her daughters. "My God! You are definitely twins. Look at the two of you!" she said, causing all three of them to laugh and cry at the same time.

* * * * *

That evening, Wilson sat back as he watched his friends try to make sense of another bizarre occurrence in their lives and welcome another unexpected daughter/sister into the fold.

Emily presented the entire story to her new family, just as she had to Wilson a few weeks earlier. This time, however, he noticed it was not as polished, nor was she as detached. It was different. It was emotionally charged, and those emotions permeated Mac and Betsy's living room. This time, she was facing the very people whose life was changed, because *her* life was changed. They were shocked and saddened as she described what happened the day she and Aimee were born, her childhood and her life with Joan as an adult. They were also proud of everything Emily had accomplished – Stanford, and Stanford Law, passing the Idaho Bar Exam, and being acknowledged as a 'rising star' in a prestigious law firm.

Watching his wife and twin daughters 'group hug,' Mac looked over at Warren, smiled and said, "Do me a favor Warren? The next time, you find one of my long lost kids… can you at least make it a boy?"

Epilogue

Black Friday. For many, the day after Thanksgiving has become retail's version of a full contact sport, with game planning so extensive, it rivaled those of many NFL teams. In the weeks leading up to Thanksgiving, the three McDonald girls convinced their mother to join them as they started a new family tradition – 'Girls Day Out!'

The surprise arrival of a new sister did not change their plans. Emily was told by her sisters, that she was joining them for a day of shopping, lunch, and a visit to a relaxing spa afterward… whether she liked it or not. The day went well, and by the time everyone returned to the McDonald home, for "Thanksgiving Dinner leftovers," Emily had been fully initiated into the family sorority.

After weeks of anxiety and hesitation over whether or not to contact Betsy, Emily could not have been happier. She was beginning to re-think her original expectations of "just letting them know she existed," and regretted having scheduled her flight home for Saturday, rather than Sunday. She truly enjoyed being part of such a fun family, and looked forward to returning for an entire week that Christmas.

Four weeks later, the family gathered for dinner and to watch that week's Patriots game versus the Broncos. Emily arrived on Christmas Eve, and looked forward to that Sunday's game. Everyone loved her visits, but when she walked into the room wearing a replica Peyton Manning Denver Bronco jersey, everyone booed. "Hey, I grew up rooting for the Broncos," she said, unfazed by the negative comments.

Jim Nance has just begun his half time review of scores around the NFL, when the front doorbell rang. Mac, comfortably seated in the new La-Z-Boy recliner he'd received for Christmas, asked his grandson Drew to get the door. Returning to the family room, Drew said, "Grandpa, Sergeant Wilson needs to see you. He has a young man he wants you to meet.

Approaching the foyer, Mac saw Wilson standing there with a freckled, auburn haired boy around Drew's age. "Wilson… I know what I told you on Thanksgiving, but you've got to be kidding me!"

Wilson laughed, saying, "No, Mac. This is Brian Smith. I've been his Big Brother for the past five years. We're heading to Boston for a Bruins game. "Do you have a minute?"

"Yeah," he said smiling. "It's the halftime report and I can't understand a word Shannon Sharpe says anyway!"

The two men laughed. Then, looking at Brian, Mac asked, "Do you like football, son?"

"I love the Patriots," the eleven year-old replied.

"Well, you're in luck in then," Mac said. "The game is one in the next room. Why don't you join my grandson, Drew, while I speak to Sergeant Wilson."

"Nice kid," Mac said, as he and Wilson watched the boy walk into the family room.

"So what's up?" Mac asked, bringing the conversation back to Wilson.

"Mac, I just wanted to let you know that I'm leaving the Harbor Point PD. In fact, I'm leaving Maine. I've been offered the Chief of Police position in Pierce, New Hampshire."

"Congratulations!" Mac said, offering a handshake. "Pierce, huh? Wow, that's way up there. I've been through there a few times. Small town. It's like something out of a Norman Rockwell illustration," pausing for effect, he then added… "Or a Stephen King novel."

"Yeah, it's a nice town, and I really need the change of scenery. I've been at HBPD too long," Warren replied. "But the real reason I wanted to talk to you, Mac, is Brian. As I said, I've been his Big Brother for the past five years. I was wondering… hoping really, that you'd be interested in taking my place. I don't want him to go back to what he had before – a string of guys who liked the *idea* of being a Big Brother, but weren't really interested in putting in *the time* to be a Big Brother."

"Can I think about it, Warren? I mean… I'm still just getting used to having two new daughters."

"Of course, I understand Mac," Wilson replied. Then, reaching into his pocket, Wilson removed a business card, handing it to his friend, saying, "Tell you what, Mac. If you decide that you're interested, call Jim McLaughlin at this number."

Looking at his watch, Wilson realized he and Brian had to get going, if they wanted to get to Boston before the first puck dropped. The two men silently walked into the family room, to see Drew and Brian enjoying the Patriots game.

"Looks like he already has a new friend, Mac," Wilson said.

"Yes, it does, Warren. Yes it does.